A DEADLY FINISH

Also by Radu Herklots

The John Tedesco Cathedral Murder Mysteries:

The Cage
Leap of Faith
The Turbulent Bishop

Short Stories:

A Salisbury Tendresse and Other Tales

Autobiography:

Home Park Heaven: A Plymouth Childhood

A DEADLY FINISH

Radu Herklots

Copyright © 2026 Radu Herklots

The moral right of the author has been asserted.

Apart from any fair dealing for the purposes of research or private study, or criticism or review, as permitted under the Copyright, Designs and Patents Act 1988, this publication may only be reproduced, stored or transmitted, in any form or by any means, with the prior permission in writing of the publishers, or in the case of reprographic reproduction in accordance with the terms of licences issued by the Copyright Licensing Agency. Enquiries concerning reproduction outside those terms should be sent to the publishers.

The manufacturer's authorised representative in the EU
for product safety is Authorised Rep Compliance Ltd,
71 Lower Baggot Street, Dublin D02 P593 Ireland (www.arccompliance.com)

This is a work of fiction. Names, characters, businesses, places, events and incidents are either the products of the author's imagination or used in a fictitious manner. Any resemblance to actual persons, living or dead, or actual events is purely coincidental.

Troubador Publishing Ltd
Unit E2 Airfield Business Park,
Harrison Road, Market Harborough,
Leicestershire. LE16 7UL
Tel: 0116 2792299
Email: books@troubador.co.uk
Web: www.troubador.co.uk

ISBN 978 1836286 035

British Library Cataloguing in Publication Data.
A catalogue record for this book is available from the British Library.

Printed and bound in Great Britain by 4edge Limited
Typeset in 11pt Minion Pro by Troubador Publishing Ltd, Leicester, UK

ONE

A Deadly Start

Mickey Hunn, the best-known cab driver in Rhyminster, with his cheery manner and a face resembling a Halloween lantern in human form, was waiting patiently by his Tower cab parked outside the Woolford Memorial Hall.

Once he had spotted his passenger, he yelled across the hall's little yard.

"Commander Foster, sir! Your carriage awaits!"

A clearly tipsy old sea dog stumbled and careered towards the awaiting vehicle, where Mickey helped him into the rear passenger seat. The Commander had been attending a wine tasting.

After a vigorous bout of seat-belt wrestling, the cabbie just about managed to secure his bulky client for the short drive back to Rhyme.

"Was it a good night, sir?"

Foster slurred his response.

"It was OK. Elsted served up some acceptable reds. That idiot Jackson stormed off, of course, and Martin Smedley did his best to stink us out…"

Mickey knew his regular clients, and so he left Foster to

chunter and mutter away to his heart's content until he was snoring loudly on the back seat.

"Home, sir!" Mickey shouted at Foster as he reached the retired officer's semi-detached house, which was about a mile north of the city centre.

Having waited to make sure that his passenger had made it safely inside, Mickey yawned, turned on Greatest Hits Radio, and headed home to his own bungalow in Derrington, his day's work done.

The following morning, Foster's neighbour, Elaine, knocked repeatedly and with increased urgency on his door. During the Covid crisis she had got used to keeping an eye on him, as he was single and elderly, and the habit had continued into the post-pandemic era.

Foster was a habitual early riser and would walk to the local Nisa store before breakfast to get his *Daily Telegraph* ('the paper'), but Elaine hadn't seen him leave the house that morning.

Sensing that something might not be right, she called 999 and asked for the police.

Foster hadn't made it to his bed on the previous evening. The police discovered him unconscious, prone on his kitchen floor.

They soon found an empty tumbler and a half-finished bottle of Madeira on the sideboard, to which was attached a label marked 'Jos Elsted, Vintner of Distinction'.

TWO

**17 St Budeaux Place, Rhyminster
One Week Earlier**

Time for a quick catch-up on the life and times of the little cathedral city of Rhyminster.

After the shocking murder of the seventy-ninth bishop, the next incumbent, the first woman in the history of the See, had been appointed. Bishop Lucy was settling in well, after a steady start, to near-universal approval.

John Tedesco was still operating his small, word-of-mouth detective agency, but his business partner Lynne had moved to Bath with her new husband and, although she still helped out remotely with corporate recruitment work, the agency now consisted of Tedesco, his eccentric PA Sally Munks and his border terrier Barker, who was, sadly, approaching late-middle age in dog years.

However, Tedesco was able to call upon the informal help of his friend Jos, who was running his burgeoning wine business from the adjoining premises.

Jos had been an invaluable witness in the case of the murdered bishop and, as Tedesco was something of an amateur wine buff, they had formed an alliance which they referred to as 'Crime and Wine'.

So we join the two old friends as they enjoy a bottle of claret at Tedesco's little mews house situated off the Cathedral Close, where they are discussing Jos's upcoming wine-tasting evening at which Tedesco will be operating as assistant to the speaker, making sure that the bottles are opened at the correct temperature and in the right order and serving the wines while Jos explains them.

"Have you heard of 'Glug, Glug', John?"

"I don't think so. It sounds awful."

Elsted giggled. "It is a ghastly name for a wine society, I grant you, but they are a well-established group based in Woolford."

Tedesco tried not to sneer. Although his sister, local TV reporter Nicky, used to live in the village of Woolford before relocating to Plymouth after her divorce, he had never taken to the place. Too many opinionated men in red trousers for his liking.

"Anyway," Jos went on, "I thought it might be helpful if I went through the different characters in the group. The runners and riders, as it were."

"Or the dramatis personae?"

"Indeed," said Jos, who was used to his friend's pedantic tendencies.

"So," he continued, "let's start with the chairman. He is one of the Drs Elphick, both GPs in the village, who don't seem to have noticed the inherent contradiction of being health professionals who encourage drinking.

"Dr Mark formed the group about fifteen years ago. Dr Sue is the secretary and keeper of the peace, as the discussions can get a bit heated, especially towards the end of the session. She is also an inveterate puzzle solver, catching up on her sudoku whenever there is a gap in proceedings. You will like them both. At the other extreme there is Greville Jackson."

"I think I met him at a barbecue at Nicky's place a while back. I seem to remember him turning up in a cloak and a fedora."

"That's our Greville. He's our frustrated thespian, went to RADA in the sixties but never fulfilled his early promise. He inherited the family pile, Woolford Grange, and spends his time boring for England with his theatrical anecdotes as well as knocking back the claret, a subject upon which he is the self-declared expert."

"Thanks for the warning. Any other oddballs you want to warn me about?"

"Let's think. Sylvia Spraggon is almost up there with Greville. Retired headmistress of a girls' school in Dorset. She doesn't take prisoners and comes out with some unfiltered right-wing stuff after one glass too many. But of course, silly me, you will know her, as she lives just across the road!

"Then there's Sylvia's polar opposite, Verity Glynde, our self-styled alternative therapist, who floats around like a Laura Ashley tribute act whatever the weather."

"How does she get on with the doctors?"

"Surprisingly well. But Sylvia loves to wind her up."

"Are there any normal people?"

"Of course. We have the stock boring couple of the group, Stephen and Rachel Lowndes. She is a partner in a small but well-regarded architects' practice and he teaches at the local primary school. They have the regulation two perfect children, both away at private school. I expect that Rachel covers the fees, as I doubt if Stephen earns very much."

"Could be a source of tension between them – the income difference?" asked Tedesco.

Jos thought carefully before offering an opinion.

"I can't say that I have noticed. They both drive the same model of car. He has a blue Honda Jazz, and she has a red one. They hilariously refer to them as Thunderbird One and Thunderbird Two. Rachel and Stephen are harmless really and never get involved in anything heated or controversial, and they are generous markers."

"The wines are marked?"

"Oh yes. The members take it very seriously. Jim and Mary Clayton are the sweeties of the society. A gentle couple who retired down here to be near the grandchildren. They used to run a small garden centre in Lancashire. Jim is always the first on his feet to propose a toast to the guest speaker in his lovely warm accent. Make sure you try Mary's award-winning chutney if she offers some."

"Will do. Is that it?"

"Not quite. I haven't mentioned Peter and Poppy LaGarde, quite clearly a deed poll job—"

"Let me interject," said Tedesco, "we call it a 'change of name deed' nowadays."

"I stand corrected, Your Honour. Anyway, I don't think you will relate well to those two, no siree. Peter and Poppy are the brash newcomers from London straight out of central casting. They like to refer to themselves as Pete and Pop, but the locals have somewhat fruitier names for them.

"If you ask Pete about his work, he will tell you that he does a bit of consultancy here, a bit of day trading there. He says he has a portfolio career. She seems to enjoy living off the proceeds and spends an inordinate amount of time at that vulgar new spa just outside Dartmouth. They are best of friends with Raj Purbani. Purbani is the MP for Rhyminster."

Jos paused to top off his friend's glass, then he continued.

"I have left the best till last. Martin Smedley. You can always spot him, as he sits alone."

"Poor chap, how incredibly sad."

"Not really. He is known as 'Martin Smelly', and with good reason. He works in the archive at the cathedral and is rarely exposed to daylight, let alone soap and water. But he knows his wine, although he does tend to get drowned out by the likes of Greville – and Foster, of course. Sorry, John, I didn't bother to mention the good Commander, as you know him so well."

"And how is the old hippopotamus these days? I haven't seen him at the cathedral recently."

"We have a new bishop who isn't exactly to his liking. Oh, and I don't think he's too thrilled by my appointment as head sidesman."

"And the new dean might also be a woman, if the rumours are correct. Oh joy."

"Indeed. So, you can see why I need reinforcements."

THREE

Glug, Glug: The Tasting

The chairman, Dr Mark Elphick, welcomed everyone to the, "Much-anticipated claret tasting, with selected wines from both banks of the Garonne. But before I hand over to the esteemed Jos Elsted, and his glamourous assistant – sorry, John! – the secretary has an item of business."

Dr Sue stood up, the epitome of brisk efficiency, channelling mid-period Margaret Thatcher in her blue silk blouse with a pussy bow.

"Thank you, Mr Chairman! I am planning the calendar for next year and several of you have suggested that we might miss out our first meeting as so many of us are doing dry January these days—"

Sylvia Spraggon sprang to her feet and interrupted. "Who suggested this? One of the woke brigade, I assume. Piffle and nonsense. We need more alcohol to get us through January, not less."

"Hear, hear!" boomed Commander Foster.

Greville Jackson rose somewhat unsteadily to add his considered thoughts.

"Do some of us need to be reminded of the old nursery

rhyme? 'Thirty days hath September, April, May and November. All the rest have thirty-one except February and January, which goes on for-fucking-ever! Let's hear no more of this limp-wristed rubbish. We are a serious drinking club, or we are nothing!"

Dr Sue reclaimed the floor. "Verity – I know you wanted to postpone the January meeting?"

The alternative therapist had only just started to talk when Foster shouted, "Speak up, woman!" at her, which prompted Jim Clayton to stand up and apply some soothing balm.

"I think some of us need to lighten the mood, Mr Chairman. Just imagine for a second what our guests must be thinking. And Mary and I think that Verity has a point. We should encourage responsible drinking at our club, and missing January does this in a very small way."

Rachel Lowndes said that she agreed with Jim, while her husband didn't have any strong feelings either way.

Peter and Poppy LaGarde always went skiing in January so didn't care if the club met or not. It was all about them, really.

"What about you, Whiffy?" asked Sylvia, addressing her question to Martin Smedley.

"I was going to vote in favour of a January tasting, but if personal remarks are being hurled in my direction, I will vote to cancel the first meeting of the year."

"Who said anything about voting? This isn't a democracy!" shouted Greville Jackson, resplendent in his embroidered waistcoat.

"I don't believe in democracy, unless the suffrage is restricted to graduates of certain Oxbridge colleges," interjected Sylvia.

The chairman glanced anxiously at his wristwatch. "We really mustn't keep our guests waiting. I sense that the feeling of the group is that most of us want to skip January, so that is what we will do."

"Bollocks," muttered Commander Foster.

"Stuff and nonsense," said Sylvia, shaking her head in disbelief.

After reintroducing Jos Elsted, the presentation began with what Jos described as a 'light warm-up number' from the Languedoc.

While his friend talked about the vineyard, the maker and the terroir, Tedesco poured small amounts of the wine into the tasting glasses that he had set up earlier.

Each table was supplied with these glasses, as well as a communal spittoon, some French bread and generous supplies of creamy butter from Rhyme Dairies.

The members swirled, sniffed, sipped and then some of them spat out to signify that they had completed the tasting.

In the case of Greville Jackson, he entertained the group to a symphony of growling and hawking noises, followed by a deep inward breath before gobbing theatrically into the spittoon.

Tedesco noticed that the women were clearly revolted by Jackson's extravagant and entitled display, especially Verity Glynde, whereas, with the exception of Martin Smedley, the men appeared to be suppressing a collective snigger.

The first tasting completed, Dr Mark took to the floor, while Dr Sue was poised to record the marks in the club's tasting book.

"So, let's go round the table. Martin Smedley?"

"I liked it. A good all-rounder, I would say. Eight out of ten."

Foster grunted something inaudible while the chairman asked Stephen and Rachel Lowndes for their scores. They both awarded six marks; they had never been known to vote other than the same way.

Jim Clayton, in the manner of the late Len Goodman, announced that he would award 'Sev-en!', whereas Mary thought the wine was a bit headachy, so she gave it a six.

Pete thought it tasted a bit cheap. "Where did you get this one, Jos – Aldi or Lidl?"

No one laughed. He marked it down to four. Pop glared at her husband. "Well, I liked it a lot, so it's nine from me!"

Verity Glynde thought that the wine had a top note of rosehip, which prompted an audible, "Bullshit," from Jackson. She gave it an eight-plus.

That left the awkward squad – Greville Jackson, Sylvia Spraggon and Commander Foster.

Jos Elsted looked like a schoolboy waiting outside the headmaster's study as he awaited Jackson's verdict.

"I thought it was…"

Jackson paused for what seemed like an age, as if he was about to announce who was about to be sent home on a reality show.

"Really rather good. Well done, Elsted. I hope this is a harbinger for what is about to come. Seven out of ten."

Sylvia was much less generous. "Weak, short, no oomph. I expect a red to be a real thruster, something that will ejaculate in my mouth with waves of fruity pleasure. This was a real let down, Elsted. Three. And that's being kind."

Foster agreed with her. "I must raise the danger signal. Weak, woolly and the nose was pure barnyard. Four."

"Ha ha, well, our team of tasters has once again produced

some interesting comments, and from the range of marks, I suppose you could say that the first wine of the evening was a bit 'marmite,'" said Dr Mark, before handing over to Dr Sue, who announced that the average mark for wine number one was a respectable 6.8.

The evening continued in similar vein. After a fifteen-minute break for food, Jos moved on to the heavier reds, which went down well with the awkward squad.

Sylvia was particularly effusive in support of wine number seven, the penultimate selection of the evening, describing it as 'hard as nails' and a wine she could imagine herself 'sucking heartily direct from the bottle to bring comfort on the coldest winter night'.

The final selection of the evening, from a small boutique estate near to the city of Bordeaux, divided opinion.

Martin Smedley admired the complexity of the structure; Pete thought it tasted expensive, always a good thing in his eyes, but nothing prepared the group for Jackson's angry outburst.

He had previous form for storming out of tastings, but his reaction to this wine was extreme even by his standards.

"Elsted, you should be taken henceforth by Commander Foster here to His Majesty's dockyard in Devonport and hung from the yard arm for serving this foul brew. It was like sewage with a top note of fresh vomit! Nil marks, and I trust that a refund will be forthcoming!"

"How do you know?" asked Stephen Lowndes.

"What!"

"Yes," Verity piped up. "Have you actually sampled sewage and fresh vomit? If not, how can you make the comparison?"

"Don't be absurd, woman! This was a blend – Australian crap if I'm not mistaken. We've been sold a pup, Elsted."

"But claret is a blend of grape varieties, as you well know, you idiot," said Martin Smedley.

"Bog off, Smelly!" was Jackson's considered riposte. Then he stood up, reattached his cape and stormed off into the night like a stage villain from a Victorian melodrama.

FOUR

Glug, Glug: The Aftertaste

After such a late night for the detective, Tedesco and his dog Barker had been a little slow to get moving the following morning.

Barker, bless him, couldn't settle down to sleep until his master's return and so it was no surprise that Sally greeted them at the office door with, "You two look as if you've had a night on the tiles!"

Half an hour later, just as he was in the middle of dictating a lengthy invoice, his PA barged in, interrupting his train of thought.

"Mr Elsted is here – shall I say you are busy?"

"Of course not, Sally. You shouldn't need to ask."

"But you looked as if you didn't want to be disturbed."

Tedesco muttered something indistinct and then wandered out to the front office, where he found his normally cheerful friend and colleague looking distinctly below par.

"Are you alright, Jos? I thought last night went very well. I wouldn't worry about Greville Jackson – nobody else does."

"You clearly haven't heard," said Jos. "Look, Sally," he

went on, "can you hold calls for a few minutes? John and I need to talk in private."

The PA's mind raced in all directions at this news, while her bosses secreted themselves in the tiny conference room.

"John. I just bumped into Wilf Drake as I was walking across Cathedral Green."

Canon Wilfred Drake, the precentor at the cathedral, was a close friend and ally of both men.

"And how was he?"

"Distraught. Elaine, his cleaner, had just called to cancel."

"I can't imagine Wilf being precious about that…"

"Elaine lives next door to Commander Foster. She didn't see him taking his daily stroll to the paper shop, so she tried the door without success, had a good snoop around outside and found no sign of movement, so she called the police."

"This doesn't sound promising."

"It isn't. He was found on the floor, stone dead."

Tedesco stood up and walked around the room, trying to take this in.

"But he seemed fine last night. His normal cantankerous self. But perhaps we shouldn't be too surprised. How old was he, eighty plus? And he was overweight, drank heavily and I doubt he was a practitioner of clean eating."

Jos smiled shyly. "He always wolfed down the sausage rolls at the sidesmen's AGM."

"Let's hope that he didn't suffer too much. I assume there will be big a funeral at the cathedral."

Jos visibly gulped. "I hadn't thought of that. It will be my first since I was voted in. Ironic or what."

Foster had been the hard-line head sidesman at the cathedral for more years than Tedesco could remember. The congregation and clergy were delighted when he reached eighty, as they assumed that he would stand down, but he insisted on remaining in place.

With the tacit encouragement of the dean and chapter – the governing body of the cathedral – Jos had forced an election, which he had won hands down. Foster had barely spoken to him since his ignominious defeat, apart from at Glug, Glug.

"I remember years back when the Commander sat me down in the refectory and told me, very seriously, that the sidesmen were the most important people in the cathedral," Tedesco recalled.

"That sounds about right."

"He explained that in the dim and distant past, the cathedral didn't have enough staff to marshal the major services – Christmas, Easter, society weddings and so on – so the Guild of Sidesmen was formed in order to recruit volunteers. They wrote their own constitution and developed various conventions over the years. You know the sort of thing: 'no one shall leave their seat during the service, no jeans, no smiling under any circumstances'. They prescribed all manner of arcane rules, hand gestures to guide people up to communion and what not."

"This explains why they've been in a thorn in the side of the dean and chapter for so long. Things will change on my watch, I can promise you," said Jos.

"That was your mandate, as I recall," replied Tedesco.

"Anyway," he continued, "I flippantly told Foster that the Mafia started out in a similar fashion, as an informal group that was set up to guard the nobles of Sicily."

"I don't suppose that the Commander was amused."

"Of course not. 'Are you comparing the Guild of Sidesmen of this fair cathedral to the Cosa Nostra? How dare you, sir!' We won't see his like again," said Jos.

"Unless you become power-crazed, old friend."

"You and Barker would soon tell me, wouldn't you?"

"Our loyalty is assured, Don Jos."

FIVE

A Complex Structure, with a Hint of Foul Play

The scene-of-crime team was already busy at work on Foster's property when DCI Julia Tagg and DS Matt Lovell arrived.

Jools Tagg had been recently promoted to Detective Chief Inspector upon the retirement of Jimmy Bloomfield, who had escaped to Norfolk to spend more time with his golf clubs.

DCI Tagg was the protégé of Tedesco's former sidekick, ex-CID officer Lynne Davey, and in recent times she had been her closest friend in Rhyminster.

The terrier-like Lovell was soon drawn to a Post-it note on Foster's fridge, which read, 'Glug, Glug – Tuesday night'.

Today was Wednesday.

"What do you think, boss?"

"I assume this refers to yesterday evening. The neighbour told the uniforms that Foster was picked up and driven off at around 7pm. She was fairly sure about the time as *The One Show* had just started."

"I always wondered who watched that. But what do you think 'Glug, Glug' refers to?"

"Hmm. Sounds like he went out for a drink or two."

"He's got plenty of booze in the house. And I've just spotted an open bottle over there."

DCI Tagg wandered over to the sideboard, taking care not to touch anything.

"This could be interesting. The bottle has a foreign label; the word 'Madeira' appears on it."

"So it's probably Portuguese."

"Oh my days. Look at this."

"What is it?"

"That sticker – 'Supplied by Jos Elsted, Vintner of Distinction'. Listen, Matt, why don't you finish up here, and I will go and pay a visit to his premises in Minster Precincts. And is it just my sensitive nose, or does this place stink to high heaven?"

*

Elsted's premises were directly above Tedesco's, in the characteristic building which the detective liked to describe as a 'medieval office block'.

As DCI Tagg made her way up the communal spiral staircase, she hesitated outside Tedesco's office and wondered about popping in for a coffee, but decided that she was on duty and that time was precious and continued up the stairs into Elsted's little empire.

Once there, she discovered Sally Munks engaged in opening a case of wine with a vicious-looking knife.

Tagg waited until Sally had completed the slitting and then greeted her warmly.

"Sally! Aren't you supposed to be downstairs?"

"I work for both of them now – the shared help! But I enjoy the variety…"

"Is Jos around?"

"You've just missed him. He's delivering to the wine shop in Totnes. Can I pass on a message?"

"Look, you may be able to answer this. Does 'Glug, Glug' mean anything to you?"

"Yes, it does actually. Jos was conducting a tutored tasting for them last night."

Noting Tagg's puzzled expression, Sally continued.

"The gluggers are a wine-appreciation society who meet in Woolford every month. John was there as well – why don't you ask him about it? He and Barker would be made up to see you."

Having escaped from Sally's determined attempt to recruit her for her latest fundraising wheeze, the DCI hurried back downstairs, where she found an excited border terrier, who had recognised her footsteps, wagging his tail with a winning enthusiasm.

She bent down to stroke him. "Hello, Barker! I haven't seen you for ages. Is the boss in?"

Barker led her into the conference room and then returned to his basket in the main office.

"Jools! I hope this is a social call – is it?"

"I need your help again. I gather that you were assisting Jos at the wine tasting in Woolford last night."

Tedesco fiddled with his tie. "I assume that this relates to the late Commander Foster."

"I am afraid so. I was hoping to see both of you – you and Jos – as we discovered something a little strange at Foster's property this morning. An opened wine bottle, with Jos's label on it. I had understood that they didn't get on – Jos and Foster – partly because of the aftermath of our last case together."

"And don't forget, Jos is about to take over as head honcho of the sidesmen."

Jools allowed herself a shy smile. "So, I won't get told off if I sit in the wrong place at the carol concert this year."

"Certainly not! But it does seem puzzling. I would have imagined that Foster replenished his cellar from another source."

"But I assume that he was happy to sample Jos's selections at Glug, Glug?"

"He was – although he was quite rude about them. Anyway, what was this opened bottle?"

"It was a bottle of Madeira. That's a fortified wine, isn't it?"

"Good knowledge, DCI Tagg. It is created by a unique process involving oxidising the wine through heating and aging."

"OK, I have never tried it myself, isn't it something old biddies used to drink?"

"I wouldn't put it quite so graphically, but it did have considerable appeal to the port-and-lemon brigade. However, it has enjoyed something of a renaissance of late, although the French still use it for cooking purposes only. But I am more than a little surprised that Jos supplied it. He never has while I have been working with him."

"Interesting. Listen, we may need you both to make statements in due course, as you would have been among the last people to see Foster alive. And do you have a list of the guests at Guzzle, Guzzle?"

Tedesco rewarded DCI Tagg with a lovely broad grin.

"It's called Glug, Glug, but I prefer your name for it. I will ask Sally to email the list over to you, but I can't offer contact details, obviously."

"Good old data protection. Oh, there was one other thing. Did Foster have awful BO?"

Tedesco mulled the question over. "No, I don't think so."

But, he thought to himself when Tagg had left, *I know someone who does.*

SIX

Sylvia

By the time she arrived back at the station, the list of attendees at Glug, Glug had landed in Julia Tagg's inbox.

She scanned through the names, recognising some of them. She hadn't been a pupil at Sylvia's exclusive school, but she was more than aware of her by reputation. Sylvia was a regular correspondent to the *Rhyminster Journal*, eloquent in her constant invective against various aspects of local life, from the cost of town-centre parking and the planned closure of the toilets in the market square to the rudeness of shop staff.

The retired head lived practically opposite Tedesco, and Julia had seen her peering through the lace curtains the last time she was there, so she decided to pay Sylvia a visit on her way home.

It was around 7pm when she squeezed into the last available space in St Budeaux Place.

Sylvia answered the door on the first ring of the bell.

"What on earth are you doing here? We can't have the Feds calling in, think of the impact on property prices!"

The normally ice-cool DCI started to respond, but Sylvia carried on.

"Don't stand outside gawping, girl! You'd better come in before the neighbours see you."

Tagg looked around the property. Tedesco's place across the road was strikingly similar from the outside, but whereas the interior design theme of number 17 was 'tidy bachelor', number 8 was a hoarder's paradise.

"Come on, come on, don't dawdle. Builder's or lesbo?"

"Er…"

"I'm offering you a cup of tea."

"Do you have camomile?"

Sylvia slapped her thigh, as if she was auditioning for the role of principal boy in the Rhyminster Christmas pantomime.

"I knew it! Lesbo it is then!"

The DCI followed Sylvia into her crowded kitchen and was immediately shooed out and told to wait in the drawing room.

This was a small reception room which Tagg's grandmother would have referred to as the parlour.

After what seemed like an eternity, Sylvia arrived with a tray bearing two chipped mugs, one containing what looked like Bovril and the other which just seemed to be a mug of hot water.

Whatever it was, lesbo tea tasted vile.

"Now, you are probably wondering how I know that you are in the fuzz. I live opposite Tedesco and his dog, definitely the brains in that outfit. I've seen you there with Bloomfield so I put two and two together."

Tagg made herself as comfortable as she could be when seated on a sofa with sharp wires protruding at various intervals.

"I am here because you are a member of Glug, Glug."

"And so you want to ask me about Foster? Well, get on with it!"

"Why would you think that?"

Sylvia put on what could just have passed as a cockney accent and looked imploringly at her guest.

"Gawd help me, miss! You've got me bang to rights? I did him in, I did."

Tagg ignored the theatrics.

"So I take it that you have heard about Commander Foster's sad death?"

"Said so, didn't I? Of course I know. I'm a sidesman at the cathedral."

You certainly are, Tagg thought to herself.

Jos Elsted had once compared the female members of the guild of sidesmen, with a surprising unkindness, to the warders in the cult eighties drama *Prisoner Cell Block H* and had referred to one of them as 'Eva Braun'.

Perhaps he had Sylvia in mind?

Julia Tagg composed herself.

"How exactly did you hear about the Commander?"

"From a variety of sources."

"Could you just humour me by being a bit more specific?"

"I saw Canon Wilfred at the early service at the cathedral this morning, then I bumped into Tedesco and Barker on their way to work. When I got back here, the WhatWhat group was abuzz!"

"And when did you last see the deceased?" Tagg asked, deliberately trying to inject some gravitas while simultaneously ignoring Sylvia's pose of ignorance about the name of WhatsApp.

"Am I about to be arrested?" asked Sylvia, before putting her hands together as if she was about to be cuffed. "I'll come quietly, dearie, it's a fair cop," she added, reintroducing her cockney fishwife.

She really was a most irritating woman.

"Of course not. You are just helping with enquiries. We will be talking to your fellow gluggers as well."

"Right then. I saw the old fool outside the hall in Woolford awaiting his taxi. He always took one from Tower Cabs."

Tagg made a mental note to have a word with Mickey Hunn.

"And what time was this?"

"I don't know. I'm not the speaking clock, you silly girl! About 9pm or so?"

"Thank you, Ms Spraggon, you have been most helpful. Just one more question, if you don't mind, then I will leave you to enjoy your evening."

"It's Miss Spraggon, as you bloody well know. 'Ms' indeed! One more question then."

"Thank you. When did you leave the club?"

"Dunno. A bit later."

Tagg's body language indicated that she had no intention of leaving without achieving more clarity from her tricky interviewee.

"Listen, cloth ears, I left at approximately 9.15pm and then I drove home in a southerly direction, arriving twenty minutes later."

"So, you decided that it was appropriate to drive home from the tasting?"

"We gob it out – the wine! And do you really think that public service vehicles run from rural outposts at that time of night? You lot are just as bad as the politicians – totally out of touch."

"Good night, Miss Spraggon. You have been most helpful."

Julia crossed the little mews and knocked hopefully on Tedesco's door, where she was greeted by Barker and then his master.

"Jools! What a pleasant surprise! Come in, please."

"I need to decompress. I have just encountered pure madness in human form."

"Sylvia? Poor you. I'd offer you a drink but…"

"I've got the car. That's fine. I could do with a strong coffee though."

The two of them took their drinks into Tedesco's cosy little den, where he kept his extensive record collection.

"Was she helpful?"

"Up to a point. What do you think happened?"

"Off the record?"

Tagg nodded.

"Foster was a heart attack in waiting."

"That was roughly what the medic said. But that bottle of Madeira?"

"I doubt if he drank much of it; at most, he might have had a nightcap. And even if he had swigged quite a bit, it wouldn't have killed him, unless it was laced with something."

"That's what I was wondering. I guess we will know soon."

"And to anticipate your question, Jos and I were the last to leave. We had to clear up, load the van with the unused and unsold stock and then we waited five minutes for Stander the caretaker to turn up and lock up. We drove back to Minster

Precincts, left the van there, then we walked to the Close before we went on our separate ways."

Julia said her goodbyes to Barker, promised to be in touch with Tedesco about his statement, assuming one would be necessary, and then she drove towards the railway station. There was an even chance that Mickey Hunn might still be around, as there were at least two trains from London still to arrive.

As she approached the taxi stand, she soon picked out the unmistakable form of Mickey, mobile phone clamped to his ear.

Spotting her as she got out of the car, Mickey ended the call – "Gotta go, love" – and gestured to Julia to come over.

"And how is my favourite officer of the law?"

"I bet you say that to all the girls. Mickey, you know everything that goes down in Rhyme. Have you heard about Commander Foster?"

"Yeah, terrible business. But he was getting on, and the size of him!"

"He was a large man, I agree."

"Huge unit."

"Indeed. Listen, did you drive him home last night?"

"You have done your homework. Yeah, I picked him up from Woolford. He'd had a few, so I was extra careful to make sure he made it to the door when we got back to his place."

"Did he say much on the journey home?"

Mickey performed some complicated facial gymnastics while he tried to remember.

"Not really. He had nodded off by the time we were back on the main road. He did mutter something about the wines being alright. Oh, and he referred to some geezer called

Jackson, I think it was. Said he was an idiot. And some bloke called Martin, who had stunk the place out."

"That could be really useful, Mickey. By the way, did you take Foster to the meeting? I'd rather assumed that you had picked him up."

"No, he made it there under his own steam, I think."

"He could have got a lift from one of the others, I suppose?"

"Yeah, I guess so. But why all the questions? He died of natural causes, surely?"

"Probably. But I need to prepare the ground in case he didn't."

Mickey looked thoughtful. "Jools," he said, somewhat plaintively. "Are you still in touch with Lynne?"

"Very much so. I'm going to stay with her and Duncan next time I have a free weekend."

"Give her my love, will you."

SEVEN

A Foggy Morning in Rhyme

As Tedesco greeted the day, he was amazed by what was revealed when he drew back the curtains. The cathedral tower had completely disappeared, as if a massive cherry picker had arrived in the night, lifted it off and taken it away.

Rhyminster, with its five rivers, was prone to fog, but this was most unusual.

Barker looked up at him expectantly, so his master agreed to a pre-breakfast walk around the Close.

"Now where's that torch?"

Barker gave him one of his 'search me, mate, I'm a dog' looks while Tedesco noisily opened and closed various drawers before remembering that he had left it in his car, the beloved Lancia.

Torch duly recovered, the two of them wandered carefully around the medieval edifice that was a daily reminder of the permanence of history, Tedesco hoping that at least one of the local photographers was up and about to record the fog-bound scene for posterity.

"Come on, old pal. You asked for some exercise, so fetch this!"

Tedesco produced Barker's favourite yellow tennis ball from the pocket of his barn jacket and hurled it towards the north walk of the Close.

Instead of returning with his toy, the border terrier began to bark with increasing urgency.

"What is it, old friend?" asked Tedesco, as he hurried anxiously towards his cherished companion.

The detective shone his torch towards the area that Barker was trying to point out to him.

"Oh no. Please no," he said to himself. "Barker, it appears that you have uncovered another suspicious death."

As he shone the torch on the body, he immediately recognised who it was. It was Verity Glynde, the alternative therapist.

*

Tedesco whipped out his phone and uniformed police were soon on their way.

Cathedral Close was cordoned off as a potential crime scene, and Tagg was soon calling Tedesco, arranging to see him in his office. She could drop by on her way to the station.

"Thank heavens I had a shower and a shave before we came out, Barker, but we both missed breakfast. I'll get Sally to arrange something at the office."

"Woof," barked a hangry Barker.

Tagg arrived five minutes after Tedesco.

Sally got the coffee going, and then Tedesco sent her out for some pastries and some kibble for Barker.

He explained to the DCI why he had been in the Close so early and confirmed the identity of the deceased. He added that Verity must have been out all night and could have frozen to death.

"She was a member of Glug, Glug as well, wasn't she?" said Tagg, rhetorically.

"How did she get on with the other members?"

"My observation was that she was a gentle soul, a bit of a new-age dreamer, so she stood out from the likes of Greville Jackson and Foster, loud-mouthed misogynists both. Oh, and she clashed with the Drs Elphick a bit."

"Because she was a holistic therapist or whatever."

"Yes, but it was fairly good-natured. Dr Mark teased her about her qualifications – where did you go to medical school, Totnes? That kind of thing. Light ribbing."

"Because Totnes is the hippy centre of Devon, I suppose. Hilarious."

"I agree. But Verity could give as good as she got, especially once she'd had a glass or two."

"And I don't suppose you know where she lived? Any family?"

"Here in the Close, one of the flats in the old teacher-training college."

"And how could she afford that, I wonder?"

"Inheritance, I'm guessing. The only family I know about is a daughter in Vermont, called Tree or maybe Twig or something equally daft. No idea who the father was."

"Thanks, John. I'd better get to work. The press will be all over this before we know it."

"I bumped into Julie Stringer the other day and she told me how boring Rhyminster had become now that the cathedral murders have stopped. How nothing interesting had happened apart from that busker who got ejected from the cathedral for regaling the morning worshippers on Easter Sunday with 'Losing My Religion.'"

Julie was the legendary reporter on the *Rhyminster Journal*, whose 'It Makes Me Mad!' column had been eagerly devoured by Rhymesiders for several decades.

"Good old Julie. Well, it seems like the old place is about to get interesting again. Look, I will be in touch with you and Jos about Foster, so if you can remember anything else…"

"You will be the first to know."

*

Once he'd fed Barker, and had wolfed down a Jenks Bakery pastry to satisfy his own hunger, Tedesco popped upstairs to see if Jos was in.

The wine merchant was hard at work on his computer but looked up eagerly when he saw his friend and colleague.

His normally cheerful demeanour vanished as soon as Tedesco relayed the sad news about Verity.

"I hope it was an accident, John, although it seems beyond coincidence that this happened so soon after Foster."

"My thoughts exactly. Oh, and I was hoping to catch you yesterday – and so was Julia Tagg, actually. Sally said you were visiting the wine shop in Totnes."

"I did pop in there first, but I spent most of the day at a foodie fair in Dartmouth, trying to whip up support for the local hospitality sector. It was in the diary, actually."

"Typical Sally carelessness! Anyway, Jools and I both wanted to talk about Foster."

"I had rather assumed that he must have had a heart

attack. But I suppose we were two of the last people to see him alive."

"It's a bit more complicated. You see, when they found the body, the police also spotted an open bottle of Madeira, which it looked as if Foster might have drank from just before he died."

"Have some Madeira, m'dear," said Jos.

"Yes, it does all sound a bit like a Victorian melodrama. But the weird thing is that the bottle was badged as if you had supplied it."

Jos scratched his nose. "But I don't supply the stuff. Never have. It tastes like cough medicine – there's no way that I'd put my name on it."

"That is what I told Jools."

"So someone else must have stuck one of my labels on the bottle. But why?"

"To divert suspicion from others perhaps? My gut instinct tallied with yours. Foster was in poor health and ate and drank way too much. It was only a matter of time before his heart gave out. And anyway, who would want to get rid of an old relic like him?"

Jos looked sheepish. "Everyone knows that he and I have never hit it off. There was the business with the last bishop, and then I deprived him of his position as head of the sidesmen."

"Which would give him a motive for getting rid of you, not the other way round."

"Good point. But how would anyone else get hold of my labels?"

Tedesco hesitated, deep in thought, before he responded to his friend's question.

"Sally and I have access to them. And they are always out on the table at Glug, Glug so we can stick them on the bottles. Could one of the members have taken a few of them when nobody was looking?"

"This all seems a bit far-fetched, John. Anyway, let's hope that the doctor certifies the death as old-age related, or a straightforward heart attack. But back to poor Verity. You don't suppose that there is a serial killer out there who wants to bump off all the gluggers?"

"It does seem bonkers, but who would have imagined the body in the chantry, and the volunteer falling off the tower, let alone the late bishop getting murdered at the evangelical festival? This place seems fated to be the scene of the most peculiar crimes."

"You know what worries me, John?" asked Jos. "If there is a madman on the loose, who is going to be next?"

*

Tagg was greeted excitedly by DS Matt Lovell as soon as she arrived at work.

The lab had tested the Madeira bottle, and a toxicology report had been ordered, the inference being that the contents might have been adulterated with another liquid. There were prints on the bottle – Foster's and one other.

If this wasn't startling enough, the uniformed officers at the scene had gained entry to Verity's flat via the caretaker and had discovered another half-empty bottle of Madeira bearing the Elsted Wines logo.

They managed to speak to two of Verity's retired neighbours, both of whom saw her leave the flat at about

10pm. One of them, who had been at a concert at the Arts Centre, had passed her on the stairs. She clearly recalled that Verity had said that she just needed to pop outside for some fresh air before turning in.

EIGHT

Helping the Police with Enquiries

"Sorry to have to do this," Matt Lovell said to Tedesco and Elsted when they reported to the Bristol Road Police Station.

"It's OK, Matt," Jos replied. "We quite understand."

"We just need to eliminate you from our enquiries. Thanks for agreeing to be fingerprinted, and for letting us see your order book – we are satisfied that you have never ordered Madeira."

"Not quite our thing, is it, John?"

Tedesco pulled a face at the very idea of it.

Once they had made their marks, the two friends and colleagues were free to leave.

"I'm really worried," Jos admitted. "Our prints could well be on those labels. That's what they think, isn't it?"

"The labels have your name on them, so they have to see if this means anything, but neither of us stuck them on a bottle of Madeira, did we? So don't worry – someone else did it. I expect they are looking into all of the participants from the tasting."

"I hope you are right. I hate this. I've never been in a police station before."

While the partners in 'Crime and Wine' awaited further developments, the police were out and about interviewing the remaining gluggers.

Julia Tagg drove out to the village of Derrington in the early evening and was rewarded by the sight of Thunderbirds One and Two parked on the driveway of Stephen and Rachel Lowndes' unremarkable seventies-style executive home on a housing estate which had a distinctly *Abigail's Party* vibe to it. It would have been considered aspirational when it was developed; now it looked dull and unloved. The world had moved on.

Stephen answered the door, seeming completely unsurprised by the unheralded arrival of a DCI on his doorstep, and then Rachel materialised out of nowhere to usher their guest into an antiseptically clean lounge.

"We know what this is about," said Stephen, Rachel nodding vigorously in support.

"In that case, you will understand why we are talking to all of the members of Glug, Glug who attended the recent tasting."

"Absolutely," said Rachel. "I was saying to Stephen earlier, wasn't I, darling, that we hope that the police will be all over this."

"Because if someone out there is harbouring a grudge against the members, we could be next," said Stephen, finishing his wife's sentence for her.

"And can either of you think of anyone who might have a grudge?" Tagg ventured.

The couple both thought for a while, then Stephen said that he couldn't imagine why anyone would have it in for a respectable group of wine aficionados.

"I agree with my husband," said Rachel. "So it must have been someone in the club. Greville Jackson would be my prime suspect."

"And why would that be?" Tagg asked, with a practised patience.

"He was always calling Commander Foster an idiot, or worse," said Stephen.

"And he couldn't stand Verity either," Rachel added. "He referred to her as a 'woke daisy chain of a nincompoop' at the Christmas party."

Tagg let the couple recount several more instances of name-calling before calling a halt to the speculation.

"Mr and Mrs Lowndes. You will understand that I do need to ask you a couple of questions, if you are happy to cooperate."

"Do we need to come to the station?" Stephen asked.

"I think you've been watching too many police dramas," Rachel went on.

"Look. You can come to the station if you prefer, but I can deal with this informally."

"Why not – fire away," said Stephen.

"Right. I just need you to let me know at what time you arrived at the tasting, what time you left and how you travelled."

The two of them confirmed that they had arrived at 7.20pm precisely, as they always did, and that they had travelled there and back in Thunderbird Two. Stephen had driven. They took it in turns so that only one of them had to spit the wine out.

The charismatic duo confirmed that they had left the tasting at 9.15pm and that they had seen Sylvia Spraggon walking to her car and Foster awaiting his taxi.

While Tagg concluded her questioning, her stolid sidekick, DS Matt Lovell, was facing the somewhat more challenging task of interviewing Greville Jackson at Woolford Grange.

Having driven his unmarked Skoda Octavia up what seemed to be a never-ending but appallingly maintained gravel drive, he came to a rotted wooden sign that read 'Woolford Gr.'.

After checking his tyres following the challenge of the rutted, potholed entrance to the ancestral home, Lovell made his way on foot towards the front door, more than a little hesitantly.

He tugged on a massive bell pull several times, and, receiving no response, he walked around the exterior of the somewhat sinister pile in search of a tradesman's entrance.

The normally unflappable detective sergeant almost jumped out of his skin when he was confronted by a large man dressed in what appeared in the dusk to be a ceremonial gown of some kind.

As the man drew closer, Lovell saw that he was wearing a Homburg hat and, even more disconcertingly, that he was pointing what looked alarmingly like a musket at him.

"And pray, what business do you have here, sirrah!" shouted the man, who fitted DCI Tagg's description of the aging thespian to a tee.

Lovell produced his warrant card and waited for Jackson to go through an elaborate routine which involved fixing his reading glasses, which were attached to a chain that he wore around his neck, before staring at his guest intently several times, comparing his face with his proof of identity. He was then grudgingly admitted into the Grange.

"Why didn't you ring the bell, you silly ass!" said Greville Jackson.

"I did."

"But did you yank it hard enough, man?"

They walked through a dusty corridor, which was notable for the various hunting trophies hanging somewhat precipitously to the walls, and then the old actor led the detective into his book-lined study.

The walls featured black-and-white photographs of various people, some of whom Lovell vaguely recognised.

Noting that his guest was distracted by these images, Greville Jackson explained that they were all members of the profession with whom he had performed.

"On the left, bitter old queens. On the right, sweet old darlings."

Before Lovell could explain the purpose of his visit, his host suddenly exploded.

"What in the name of Larry and Rafe! Leave the room at once!"

An old black Labrador emerged from under Jackson's desk and trudged dolefully towards the French windows that gave out onto the overgrown lawn.

"Smollett's just farted!" Greville announced by way of explanation. "Anyway. Why are you here, Inspector Love?"

"It's Detective Sergeant Lovell, sir."

"Have you ever trodden the boards? You look familiar."

Ignoring this, Lovell got down to business.

"I am here in connection with the sad death of the late Commander Foster. I believe that you knew him and that you were one of the last people to see him alive."

"Man was a complete idiot. Nothing sad about it. One less cretin in the world – no bad thing!"

"Er, thank you, sir, but what I really need to know is when you last saw him and how he seemed to you."

"He seemed to me to be a fatuous, pompous, tedious excuse for a human being. That answer your question?"

Lovell struggled to maintain his calm. "Sir, I need specific answers."

"Well, ask me some specific questions then!"

"Are you a member of Glug, Glug?"

"You know I am. Next!"

"You were at the recent tasting at the village hall?"

"Yes, yes, get to the point!"

"What time did you arrive?"

"The normal time."

"Humour me. When is the normal time?"

"About 7.30pm. I never get there early. Can't be doing with idle chit-chat. Just want to get down to the serious business of sampling the wares."

"And how did you travel to the meeting?"

"What a bloody stupid question! On Shanks's pony, obviously. I'm hardly going to drive for one hundred yards, am I? Especially if I'm drinking!"

"And when did you leave?"

"The next morning."

Lovell wondered if he should warn Jackson that he was in danger of being charged with wasting police time. The man was quite unlike anyone he had ever met, and he had come across some real collector's items in his time.

"At the end of the tasting, of course! Why are you lot so bloody literal?"

"And did you see the deceased as you left? Did you have any words with him?"

Jackson pondered and then recalled that he had in fact left the meeting early that night.

"And why was that, sir?" asked Lovell.

"Martin Smedley. Odious little archivist from the cathedral. Stinks to high heaven, up there with the fruitiest of Smollett's farts. He had the temerity to call me an idiot, so I left the room."

Lovell, deciding that he was going to get no further, asked Jackson to contact him if he recalled anything else. He didn't mention Verity Glynde.

Jackson would obviously claim that he was in Woolford on the night in question, although he would need some corroboration if they found anything else to link him to her death.

As he handed over his card, the detective raised the question of the firearm that had been pointed at him upon his arrival at Woolford Grange.

"Of course I don't have a licence! Don't need one! It's a prop, Inspector Love, a prop!"

DS Lovell made his way back to the car, taking extra care to avoid the potholes as he drove back down the gravel drive, which was even more treacherous in the dark.

NINE

The Investigations Continue

The following morning, Lovell had the somewhat easier task of visiting the Claytons, Jim and Mary, who also lived in the village of Woolford.

Both retired, they had 'all the time in the world' to spare for the police.

The Clayton residence was a thirties bungalow on a large plot, which meant plenty of room for a garden.

A smiling Mary Clayton greeted him at the door.

"Good morning, Officer. Do come in and make yourself at home while I fetch Jim. He's always in the garden, or the greenhouse. Gardening is our life, you see. Used to run a garden centre near Clitheroe. Sorry, listen to me wittering on. I expect you knew that. Jim! You are keeping the officer waiting!"

"Half a mo, love. I'll just clean meself up."

While Jim went at it with the Pear's soap and the nailbrush, Mary offered refreshments, Lovell diplomatically choosing the gardener's tea over the coffee option.

Once the spruced-up Jim had appeared, Mary led them into the conservatory.

Lovell, not possessed of green fingers, nevertheless

managed to give a convincing performance of someone who was endlessly fascinated by raised beds, pricking out and Jim's prize-winning marrows before he gently called an end to the horticultural musings.

"Ignore my husband, DS Lovell," said Mary, in a tone of loving exasperation, "once you let him loose on the Horticultural Society show, you can't stop him.

"Jim!" she went on. "Let the poor man do his job!"

Lovell smiled. He rather liked these two. They reminded him of his late grandparents.

"That's quite alright. And this tea is lovely, by the way. Now, you both know about the two deaths of members of Glug, Glug of course."

The Claytons, sitting together on a rattan sofa, nodded vigorously.

"I need to ask you to confirm a few things."

"To rule us out, like," said Jim Clayton.

"Jim!" said Mary.

"Your husband is correct, Mrs Clayton. We just need to check a couple of points with you. So, what time did you arrive at the tasting, and how did you get there?"

A chastened Jim gestured to Mary to answer.

"We like to get there a bit early, to bag a table near the front and to catch up with our friends. We always walk there. You can see the hall from here."

"Thank you. And how was the evening? Anything out of the ordinary happen?"

Jim jumped in. "Mr Elsted produced some cracking bottles. We brought a few samples home with us after. I do remember one thing, mind. Greville Jackson stormed out just before the end."

"He did," said Mary, corroborating her husband's evidence. "Nothing unusual, he often goes off on one of his little rants. Greville used to be on the stage, you know."

"Aye," Jim added, "and this time it was poor Martin Smedley who copped it. It's normally the Commander. He and Greville really don't like each other."

"That's just about it for now. Just a couple of questions about Verity Glynde."

Mary looked to be on the verge of tears.

"It was terrible to lose the Commander, but it was no surprise really. But that lass! She was the same age as our Valerie. Doesn't bear thinking about."

"It's OK, take your time," Matt said. "Where were you both after the tasting?"

"We came back here, of course," said Jim. "We had a nightcap, one of the clarets that Mr Elsted brought with him."

"That's fine, Mr Clayton. I do need to ask."

"We understand," Mary interjected, "and can I mention something? Greville Jackson was very rude to Verity that night as well."

"I remember!" Jim said. "It was when we were looking at whether to have a meeting in January – we decided not to as it's too soon after Christmas."

"And," Mary added, "some of us give up drink in the New Year."

"Dry January," said Lovell ruefully. "I tried it this time but didn't get past the first week. So how did Ms Glynde react to Mr Jackson's outburst?"

"She gave as good as she got," was Jim's view.

"But I could tell that she was hurt," said Mary.

Lovell left it at that, slipping Mary his card in case either of them remembered anything else. She gave him a jar of chutney in return.

As he drove back to the office, the detective sergeant considered the key point he had picked up in the last few hours.

Jackson had clashed in public with Commander Foster and Verity Glynde and now they were both dead.

Meanwhile, Lovell's boss was deep in the bowels of the cathedral archive, interviewing Martin Smedley.

Jools had arrived at the cathedral just before it opened to the public and, having persuaded the jobsworth at the desk that she had legitimate business with one of the staff, and that yes, she really was a police officer, she had to edge past a gaggle of sash-wearing tour guides who were blocking the aisle.

As she wandered towards the archive, hidden away at the far end of the building, she pondered whether there was a collective noun for the groups of elderly volunteers who kept the place going.

'A threat of sidesmen' maybe, or a 'gallimaufry of guides' perhaps?

Her uncharacteristic bout of whimsy ended when she was admitted to the archive by a cathedral verger. She was immediately rewarded by a stench that could mean only one thing – male body odour.

As it was a windowless, airless part of the building that housed the archive, the putrid smell seemed to physically attach itself to the walls.

Trying not to gag, she was led to a tiny cubbyhole where she was introduced to Martin Smedley.

"Mr Smedley," she said, as breezily as she could manage in the circumstances, "I'm DCI Julia Tagg."

"I have been expecting you," said Smedley.

"Splendid! Why don't we get some fresh air and find a quiet place in the cloisters?"

The cloisters were situated near the refectory, and so there were some outside tables and chairs that could be brought into play if the inside was full.

It was quiet at that time of the morning, so Tagg was soon able to identify a spot where she and her interviewee could speak openly without fear of being overheard.

The other advantage of the cloisters was that there was a cooling breeze there which, to a limited extent, deodorised the worst of Smedley's noxious excesses.

"Mr Smedley. Let's start, shall we?"

"I know why you are here. You are interviewing all of the members of Glug, Glug about the Commander and poor Verity. Sylvia Spraggon told me to expect a visit."

Tagg made a mental note to have another word with the excitable ex-headmistress, and then she commenced her questioning.

"Martin – can I call you Martin? You live in Rhyminster, I understand."

"That's right. And, anticipating your next question, I drove myself to Woolford and back. I don't imbibe the wines, I use the spittoon, so I was perfectly sober when I drove home."

Resisting the temptation to ask him to let her do her job, Tagg asked Martin if there had been any issues between the members of the club on the night in question.

"I called Greville Jackson an idiot."

"And why would that be?"

"He was talking nonsense about wine. And he referred to me as 'Smelly', which was bloody rude of him. And then he stormed out."

"And was Mr Jackson rude to anyone else?"

The institutionalised archivist thought for a moment.

"He was rude to Foster – nothing strange there, those two hated each other's guts – but he was horrid to poor Verity, which was unforgivable."

"Thank you, Martin. And on the subject of Ms Glynde—"

"Where was I on the night of her death? At home in bed. And I don't have an alibi, unless you are prepared to accept the evidence of my cat, Perkin."

TEN

Zoom, Zoom

Tagg and Lovell divvied up the remainder of the survivors of the Glug, Glug membership between them.

Lovell took Peter and Poppy LaGarde, while the DCI arranged to meet the Drs Elphick at their surgery, after hours.

Pete and Pop proved to be somewhat tricky to track down, but Lovell managed to get hold of their housekeeper, who overcame her instinctive reluctance to disturb her wealthy employers once the detective sergeant mentioned the concept of obstructing the police in the course of their enquiries.

The LaGardes were enjoying some downtime, as the housekeeper put it, in the Bahamas.

After a certain amount of pushing and pulling, Lovell was able to negotiate a time when they could be available for an informal interview on Zoom.

It was 10pm UK time, 6pm local time, when Pete and Pop entered the conversation that Lovell had set up.

He couldn't tell whether the couple were actually on a yacht or if they had set up a background for the call, but, in either case, he refused to be distracted or intimidated.

The formalities were swiftly dispensed with – they had arrived at Glug, Glug at about 7.20pm, and they had been driven there by their housekeeper, Emma, who also acted as occasional chauffeur. She had picked them up at the end of the evening and driven them home.

There had been no one else in the car park when they left. Lovell could check this out later with the all-knowing Emma.

Poppy burst into tears when asked about Verity Glynde, claiming that this was the first she had heard about her sad passing.

Pete told Lovell that they had flown out from Heathrow the following evening and hadn't paid any attention to any local news reports.

"So, Mr LaGarde," said the DS, "if you didn't hear about Verity, how come you knew about Commander Foster, as they both appear to have died on the same evening?"

Poppy butted in. "We heard about the Commander on the Glug, Glug WhatsApp group," she explained, "but we deliberately haven't logged on since we left for the airport."

"We are having a digital detox," said Pete, "or we were until you insisted on getting hold of us."

"Couldn't it have waited till we got home – it's only another week?" bleated Poppy.

These two were beginning to try Lovell's patience.

He reminded them that two people in the group had died in suspicious circumstances, and that in order to investigate these deaths, and to prevent any further incidents, they should understand that the police needed to talk to all of the surviving Glug, Glug members.

This had the desired effect. Pete visibly winced at the

mention of the word 'surviving', and Poppy completely changed her tune.

"So what more can we do, Officer? And we expect you to work around the clock until you discover who is behind this."

"I assume we will have twenty-four-hour police protection," Pete added. "I don't need to remind you – me and Pop are very big players."

"And," Poppy interjected, "we are personal friends of our MP and the chief constable."

Batting these comments aside, Lovell asked them if they remembered anything noteworthy from the ill-fated wine tasting.

"That Greville Jackson, he was in a foul mood," said Poppy. "He was so rude to poor Verity. I can't believe she's gone! She was my therapist!"

"Jackson's your man, I reckon," was Pete's instant opinion. "He had a barney with Foster as well and left early after Smelly called him an idiot."

Lovell, through visibly gritted teeth, thanked them both for their help and asked them to contact him if they remembered anything else.

"And enjoy the rest of your holiday."

"It's not a holiday!" Poppy whined.

"My mistake – digital detox. I do apologise, Mrs LaGarde."

Earlier that evening, Julia Tagg had undertaken what was, on paper, the far more straightforward task of interviewing the husband-and-wife medical duo, Mark and Sue Elphick, respectively chairman and secretary of Glug, Glug.

The surgery had just closed for the day when Tagg pulled into the car park at 6.30pm.

The Elphicks were charming and eager to assist.

Sue told the DCI that she was arranging counselling for any of the members who wanted it, and that she and Mark had offered to help the grieving families in any way they could.

"I'm sure they all appreciate your concern," Tagg said, trying not to giggle at the likely reaction of Greville Jackson and Sylvia Spraggon to the offer of grief counselling.

The doctors were also resident in Woolford, and they confirmed that they had gone home once the village hall had been locked up and headed straight to bed.

However, they seemed a bit less certain when it came to answering direct questions about their respective arrivals and departures at the tasting.

They agreed that they had each driven in their own cars – that Sue had driven from the surgery and Mark, somewhat hesitantly, remembered that he had travelled via Rhyminster General.

"Did you go straight to the village?" Tagg asked Sue, who looked a little thrown by the question, before replying that she must have done, adding that she always arrived early in order to get there before the wine experts and to make sure they had all they needed for the tasting.

They both agreed that they had stayed later than most of the group, to make sure that the place had been left tidy for the caretaker.

Finally, they confirmed what the others had said about Greville Jackson's behaviour.

"Entre nous, Inspector," said a suddenly smarmy Dr Mark, "Sue and I wonder whether Glug, Glug needs members like Jackson. More trouble than they are worth."

"And off-putting to newcomers," said Sue, before she made Julia an offer she could readily refuse.

"Have you ever thought about joining us, DCI Tagg?"

ELEVEN

Reviewing the Situation

"So," Julia Tagg began the impromptu meeting, "Matt and I have interviewed all of the surviving members of Glug, Glug. Jade, I'll get you up to speed on our way to see Mr Jackson."

Jade Sennen had recently joined the CID from uniformed duty. A local recruit from just over the Cornish border, Tagg rated her highly and was reminded of herself at a similar stage in her career.

"Matt, any thoughts at this stage?"

"To state the obvious, the fingerprint and toxicology reports are going to be interesting, and on what we have so far, Greville Jackson is emerging as a person of interest."

"The other gluggers seem to be lining up to blame him, that's for sure."

"But," Matt noted, "we need to avoid the lazy assumption that these deaths were suspicious. Foster was old and unfit, and Verity could simply have locked herself out and died in the freezing cold."

"Yeah," said DCI Tagg, "good point, but there are too many coincidences here. They were both at the same meeting just before they died; the half-empty Madeira bottles were discovered at their respective addresses."

Jade Sennen put her hand up, as if she was still at primary school. Tagg made a mental note to have a word with her about this later.

"Ma'am, can I ask something? What is Madeira exactly?"

Lovell, smiling, joined in and explained that it was a fortified wine from the island of Madeira, which was part of Portugal.

"Is it something old people might like? Because I googled Verity Glynde last night, and she was quite young, wasn't she? And she seemed to be, how can I put this, quite a cool person, into alternative lifestyles and so on. Not someone who would be a Madeira drinker, perhaps?"

Tagg, trying not to show too much obvious pride in her protégé, simply turned to DS Lovell and said, "DC Sennen makes a good point, no?"

Lovell nodded and then continued.

"So what have we really got so far? It looks as if Elsted supplied the Madeira, but if it had been contaminated, I would look elsewhere to see who supplied the poison. The doctors would have access to all sorts of drugs, but that would be too obvious. Peter and Poppy LaGarde bother me."

"Because they are self-important, loads-of-money types down from London?"

Sennen tried and failed to hide a smirk.

"Well, yes, they are difficult to warm to, and I've done the unconscious bias courses, so I get what you are saying, but doesn't it strike you as rather too convenient that they take off for the sun just as the two bodies are found?"

"Fair point. And I too have to be aware of unconscious bias when I bring up my first interviewee."

"Sylvia Spraggon!"

"The very same. Jade, you will come across Sylvia quite a lot while you are with us. She sounds off in the local paper. On the surface, she is very aggressive, difficult and eccentric, and whatever you do, do not accept an offer of what she refers to as lesbo tea, but she is, despite appearances, sharp as a tack. I think that she knows more than she is letting on."

"She sounds lovely," said Sennen, grimacing. "And the wine company that presented the session? Do you think one of them could be involved?"

"Difficult to imagine. John Tedesco is, as I think you know, a private detective and a personal friend, so if he does become a person of interest then I will have to recuse myself. Jos Elsted runs the wine business with John's help. He has already shown us the books and, unless he has fiddled them in some way, he doesn't deal in Madeiran wines."

"What about Mr and Mrs Dullsville?" asked Lovell.

"Stephen and Rachel Lowndes? They gave nothing away, but don't forget the first rule of detective work, which is, DC Sennen?"

"It's the quiet ones who need watching."

"Exactly. So that just leaves us with Martin Smedley and the Claytons. Matt?"

"Jim and Mary were lovely. Really eager to help, and they were the only people I saw who seemed genuinely upset by what had happened. We should be able to rule them out pretty quickly."

"Hmm," said DCI Tagg, sounding doubtful, before continuing. "OK, Martin Smedley. First impressions: he stinks, so always make sure that you interview him outside. Someone in the cathedral needs to have a serious word with him. I do have concerns about Martin. Foster's flat stank as well. I wonder if Smedley was a regular visitor."

She turned to the keen new recruit.

"Jade, Foster had a senior voluntary role in the cathedral, and Smedley worked there, so they would have known each other outside the tasting club. Right! DC Sennen, you and I will go and see Greville Jackson. Matt, chase up the fingerprints and the lab report."

TWELVE

An Interesting Discovery

Tagg, breaching the unwritten rule that the junior officer drives, let Sennen into the passenger seat and headed off to Woolford.

There was heavy traffic approaching the Trago Mills roundabout, so she had plenty of time to brief her junior colleague.

Explaining that this was a follow-up to Lovell's interview, and that Jackson's participation was on an entirely voluntary basis at this stage, Tagg revealed that what she really wanted to see was the inside of Greville Jackson's wine cellar.

"To find out if he has any Madeira, I assume. But don't we need a warrant?"

"We would do if we were conducting a formal search of the premises. But we are not. And there are other ways of persuading someone like Jackson to show us what we want."

Sennen looked thoughtful. "I was wondering – flattery, showing an interest in the person's hobbies and so on?"

Tagg smiled to herself. Jade Sennen was very promising.

Once the traffic jam had eased, they travelled in companionable silence, only broken when Sennen asked about the playlist that Tagg was listening to.

"Oh, I call it 'Tedesco's Tunes'. As well as being a very good private detective – and that is very rare – he is a music buff and he's introduced me to all sorts of old stuff that I'd never heard of."

"I like this one – what is it?"

"It's called 'Home Thoughts From Abroad' by Clifford T. Ward."

Just as the song ended with a deliberate nod to Vaughan Williams's 'A Lark Ascending', they were turning into the private road leading to Woolford Grange.

"Lovell warned me about this – he wasn't wrong. Even if Jackson isn't involved in the Glug, Glug affair, he ought to be prosecuted for the dangerous state of his driveway."

Forewarned by Lovell, Tagg gave the bell pull an almighty yank, which had the desired effect. Jackson was soon to be heard clumping loudly towards the door while simultaneously shouting at someone called Smollett to sit down.

This time, Jackson was dressed in a three-piece tweed suit with a fussy waistcoat which came with its own set of lapels. The suit, like its owner, had seen better days.

Before Jackson could speak, Tagg quickly introduced herself and explained that this was just a follow-up from the visit of DS Lovell.

The old thespian seemed more interested in eyeing up Jade, which Tagg noticed straightaway.

"This is my colleague, DC Jade Sennen. Can we come in? This won't take long."

Jackson, distracted by the attractive younger woman, led them through the same corridor which he had taken Lovell down on the previous evening.

Sennen was disgusted by the stuffed hunting trophies but managed not to show it.

Smollett, as it turned out, was a black Labrador.

"I'll just let him into the garden. Smollett, out, sir!"

The poor dog looked crestfallen as he slunk into the long grass outside. He was probably looking forward to meeting some new pals.

Jackson signalled for his visitors to join him in the study.

"Have either of you trodden the boards? No? Oh well. Now, why are you here? I told Inspector Love everything I knew yesterday."

"Indeed you did," Tagg agreed. "And DS Lovell was very grateful for your help. As you may have heard, there has been another death among the members of Glug, Glug and so we are asking the remainder of the group if they have any information that might help us. It does seem to be a strange coincidence that Commander Foster and Verity Glynde were both members of your club."

As it turned out, Tagg's subterfuge was not required, as Greville Jackson leapt to his feet and announced that he needed a drink.

"This is a shock! Poor Verity! She was away with the fairies most of the time, but why would anyone want to end her life?"

"I'm sorry, sir," Tagg said, in her best emollient tone. "We had assumed that you knew."

"Well I didn't! I don't own a television, and I don't do so-called social media! Bloody hell! I need that drink. Would either of you ladies care to join me in a glass of Madeira?"

Sennen smiled sweetly at him.

"We can't have a drink because we are on duty, but I would love to see your wine cellar, if I may? My boyfriend and I are both really interested in wine and you must know plenty about it."

Twenty or so minutes later, just as Tagg was beginning to wonder if back-up was required, Sennen reappeared with Jackson, seemingly unharmed.

Jackson grabbed a glass from an ancient, dust-covered sideboard and poured himself a large measure.

"You should try Madeira, ladies. It's perfect for these cold, frosty Devon mornings. Now, have you any more questions?"

Tagg looked across at Sennen before replying. "The news about Verity was clearly a shock, so we will leave it there, but if you can think of anything that might assist us, please get in touch."

"I will. I have Inspector Love's card on the mantelpiece. Let me get Smollett safely inside before he bothers you on your way out."

Once they were off the rock-infested driveway, Tagg said that the Madeira bottle produced by Jackson might have looked a bit different from the ones found at Foster and Verity's respective homes.

"I used my phone to take some pictures in the cellar when Mr Jackson was crawling about on his hands and knees down there and none of the Madeira bottles had any label advertising Mr Elsted's firm."

"Interesting. Well done. So now we know that Jackson likes his fortified wine, we need to find out who supplies it. Hang on."

The hands-free phone was buzzing urgently.

"Tagg."

"Ma'am. It's Matt. Can you both see me as soon as you get back? I've spoken to the lab, and the results are interesting, to put it mildly."

THIRTEEN

A Toxic Brew

Lovell was waiting for them both in the incident room.

He explained that Jos Elsted's fingerprints were an exact match for some found on the Madeira bottles at both locations.

Commander Foster's prints were discovered on his bottle, but Verity had left no impression on the one that had been found in her flat.

Tedesco's prints were not present at either site.

Tagg gave a sharp intake of breath. She said, "Jos Elsted. Surely not."

"It gets more interesting, ma'am. The toxicology report shows that each of the bottles of Madeira had been adulterated with poison."

"And?"

"Preliminary results suggest that it was pure liquid prussic acid."

"Which is found in cyanide."

"That's right. Cyanide poisoning can cause dizziness, a fast heart rate and slowness of breath."

"And a strong dose can induce a coma."

Sennen spoke up. "So, for argument's sake, as Commander Foster was old and in poor health, it could have killed him, but poor Verity would have felt dizzy and might have fainted."

"It's possible, Jade, but we shouldn't speculate. Matt, I'm afraid we will have to get Jos back and interview him under caution. I wouldn't describe him as a close friend, but I do know him – and let's not forget, he is an associate of John's, so it will have be you.

"Listen, Jade, I want you at the interview with Matt. Jos Elsted needs to explain the fingerprints."

"Yes, ma'am. But what about the poison?"

"You might want to find out if he reads Agatha Christie."

Lovell and Sennen both looked puzzled.

"It's one of her best crime novels – *Sparkling Cyanide*."

*

Later that afternoon, Lovell and Sennen drove to the Cathedral Close.

They had chosen to do so as it was a short step from the Close to Minster Precincts. There was barely any room to park in the courtyard there, especially if Jos's delivery van was blocking it, and their arrival would be less conspicuous if they didn't try and squeeze past.

Sally Munks, who now worked for both Tedesco and Elsted, would be sure to spot them if they did.

Having convinced the man in the traffic warden's hut (whose job it was to prevent unauthorised parking in the refined confines of the cathedral) that they had legitimate business in the area, Lovell found a space in the North Walk.

He sent Sennen off to Elsted's office, where she would see

if the delivery van was in the yard and would then call him for further instructions.

After five minutes, Jade was able to report that the van was in situ, so Lovell told her to wait outside the little post office just around the corner where she would have a view of the yard, so she could tell him when Elsted emerged.

It didn't take too long. Sennen recognised the wine merchant from the photo on his website. She called Lovell, and they both arrived in the yard just as Jos was about to drive off on his latest delivery run.

"DS Lovell, isn't it? What brings you to our medieval office block? I'm afraid John is out at the moment."

"It's you we need to talk to, Mr Elsted. We need to ask you a few questions, so please could you accompany myself and DC Sennen here to the station. We are parked in the Close."

"That's very discreet of you. But this sounds alarming? Do I need legal representation?"

"We will deal with any questions in the station, sir," said Jade Sennen.

"But what about my deliveries? I have a responsibility to my clients!"

"And you have a responsibility to society, sir," said the eager Jade.

"Of course, of course. I want to help you as much as I can."

"Look, I'm sure we can let you get back to your business with the minimum of delay," said Matt, more reassuringly.

"We are parked just over there, in front of the Rhyminster Museum."

Half an hour later, Sally looked out of her window and

noticed that the van was still in the yard and that Jos was nowhere to be seen.

Having tried his mobile, and been transferred voice mail, she was anxiously cuddling Barker and wondering if she should report Jos as a missing person, when Tedesco arrived in the nick of time.

Over at the station, Jos had been thanked for agreeing to further questions. Lovell explained that, in the light of new information, it would be helpful to go through certain matters with him.

"You are free to leave at any time, you are not being charged, but I will have to caution you as to any evidence you give today and we will be recording the interview."

"That all seems in order. I have nothing to hide."

"Thank you, Mr Elsted. Now, do you want a solicitor present?"

"No, I don't think so."

"If you change your mind, then you can ask at any time."

"And I am free to go?"

"Yes."

Having introduced the parties for the benefit of the tape and gone through the basic formalities, Lovell reminded Jos that he had consented to be fingerprinted.

"Because of that bottle of Madeira with my logo on it," said Jos, betraying understandable nerves.

"Indeed. We have new information. Your fingerprints matched some of those found on the bottle. Can you explain why this might be?"

Jos began to sweat. "Well, no, not really. I don't sell Madeira, you know that. Look, can I see the bottle?"

"Of course."

There was a short delay while Lovell explained for the tape that the bottle had been produced, referring to its number in the evidence file.

Although it was in a see-through evidence bag, Jos knew right away that the bottle was one of his, but that this wasn't the whole story.

"Officers, I do recognise the bottle. But it isn't a Madeira bottle; this is a wine bottle."

Lovell gestured to Sennen; she could ask the next, obvious question.

"Mr Elsted, what is the difference between a standard wine bottle and one that contains Madeira?"

She remembered that the bottles in Jackson's cellar seemed a bit different from the ones found at the crime scenes.

"A bottle used for fortified wines like Madeira, and for dessert wines, is generally shorter than a standard red- or white-wine bottle. It often has a longer neck."

Conscious of avoiding the risk of the inexperienced officer putting words into the interviewee's mouth, Lovell took over.

He said, "A similar bottle was found, opened, at the home of Verity Glynde. And, again, your fingerprints were on it."

"I have no comment," said the perplexed wine merchant, before adding that he was shocked to hear this.

"Thank you, Mr Elsted. Two more questions and then DC Sennen here will drive you back to your premises. Firstly, where were you on the night of the wine tasting?"

"I drove the van back to Minster Precincts with John Tedesco, and then we walked into the Close together. John veered off towards the South Gate as he lives just the other side of it, and I continued along the North Walk to my apartment, where I spent the night, as usual."

"Did anyone see you get home?"

"I doubt it."

"Thank you, Mr Elsted. Finally, I need to ask this. Do you have any access to poisonous substances?"

FOURTEEN

Two Friends Meet in St Budeaux Place

By the time that Jos had been dropped back from the police station, the office at Minster Precincts was closed but, as the van was already loaded, he decided that he may as well carry out his deliveries.

After all, they were all local and, as Sylvia Spraggon was on his list, he decided that she would be the final stop. She would cut up about his being late, but her proximity to Tedesco's house meant that he could also call in on his colleague and his favourite border terrier.

It was 7.30pm by the time he turned into St Budeaux Place. He found a space behind Tedesco's car and parked very carefully. John was the most equable of men, but he loved his Lancia almost as much as he loved Barker.

"Oh, and now he arrives!" was the retired headmistress's warm greeting. "Well, bring it in then, come on, don't leave a girl dying of thirst."

Jos brought the wine into the crowded kitchen. Sylvia had a standard monthly order: two cases. A case of a New Zealand Sauvignon Blanc, which Jos didn't rate but was more than happy to supply, and, for the red case, an unsubtle blend of South African grapes which was branded, without apparent irony, as The Stonking Red.

"So, while you uncork a bottle of Stonker for me to taste, tell me why you are so bloody late! That drippy assistant couldn't tell me where you were!"

Jos thought quickly. "Yes, well, Sally couldn't help because I'd had a flat tyre and it was in the middle of nowhere."

"Really! Oh well. Now pour the wine, man!"

Once his customer had confirmed that the wine was drinkable, Jos practically ran across the road, where his knock on the door of number 17 brought Barker rushing to see who it was.

Tedesco soon answered and Barker gently prodded Jos with his paw as if to say, 'Come on, give me a stroke, it's good for your mental health'.

As if to prove this, Jos bent down and stroked the little terrier and told him what a good dog he was.

Barker followed the humans into the snug and found a place to hunker down in front of the wood burner.

Tedesco gestured for his friend to take a seat.

"I've just been finishing off one of the opened bottles of that St Emilion that we introduced to Glug, Glug. It's very, well, gluggable. Glass?"

Jos nodded.

"And you look as if you haven't eaten. I can offer you half of a Waitrose moussaka if you like. I can soon heat it up in the microwave."

"Please. I've had the day from hell."

"It sounds like it. Sally was about to send out a search party. So, how was the interview?"

The gentle wine merchant gulped. "How did you know?"

"I called the station."

"And they told you I was there?"

"They didn't deny it! And I assume you were told not to mention the interview to anyone. So, tell me about it."

Jos, somewhat hesitantly at first, ran through the questions he had been asked.

Tedesco got up, stretched and then sat down again, a sure sign that he was doing some serious thinking.

"So," he said, once Jos had finished, "your prints are on the bottles, but not mine. That isn't good. But the bottles contained a mix of Madeira and poison, neither of which you would have access to. And they were standard wine bottles. So, someone, or some people, are trying to point the police in your direction. It must be one of the gluggers."

"I fear that you may be right. But why would they want to kill two very different people? And will there be any more victims?"

Tedesco said, "I don't know the answer to either of those conundrums yet, but I do have a couple of questions for you. But first, let me get you that moussaka. And a top-up. Don't worry, you can leave the van here overnight. It is very safe."

Jos wolfed down the moussaka in the manner of the starving convict in *Great Expectations*.

Once he'd cleared the plate, Tedesco put his points to his friend. He said, "I was going over what happened when we got back from the tasting. You parked the van at the office then we walked back through the Close together."

Jos nodded.

"And then we split off when we got to the museum?"

"That's right. I headed on down the North Walk and you went on to the South Gate and then here."

"I think Wilf Drake saw me. He was drawing his curtains and waved."

Jos looked up eagerly and said, "If he saw both if us…"

"Then it gives you the makings of an alibi. I will go and see the canon precentor tomorrow. I haven't been to morning prayer for a bit. While I'm there, I will ask Wilf if he has any news on a date for Foster's funeral. I assume the body can be released now they have established the cause of death."

Jos gulped again. "John!"

"What is it, old friend?"

"It's hit me again! This will be my first funeral as head sidesman!"

"And I'm sure that it will go splendidly. Now, my other point. Did I or did I not see you leaving Sylvia's house before you called in here?"

"I was delivering her monthly order."

"I expect she was desperate for her Stonker. I saw her standing in the road when I got in. I expect that she was checking to see if there was any sign of your van. I explained to her that you had been unavoidably detained – not where, of course – and then she asked whether Peter LaGarde had ever tried to sell me a timeshare."

"Go on."

"Sylvia had happened to mention to Peter at one of the tastings that she had just returned from a holiday to – go on, guess where – Madeira. Walking the levadas. Anyway, Pete mentioned that he was involved in a timeshare company and that he could find her something special. He boasted that he was very well connected in Funchal, the capital."

"That's funny. He tried to sell me a timeshare once – somewhere wildly non-PLU like Tenerife or Lanzarote."

Tedesco laughed. Jos still peppered his conversation with outdated acronyms from the 1950s, or possibly earlier. PLU – People Like Us.

"Really?" he said. "I expect he knows better than to try it on with a retired lawyer like me. Anyway, poor Sylvia is still being bombarded with brochures and emails and has asked me to have a word with Pete. So I have formed an idea."

"Pray tell."

"Do you think you and Sally can hold the fort for a short while? I could do with a break, and it's quite easy to fly to Madeira at relatively short notice these days. I think it might help the investigation. There are two Madeiran angles: the wine and now a possible timeshare connection. This can't be mere coincidence. And I'm sure that my sister would house-sit and look after Barker for me."

"Knowing Nicky, she'd jump at the chance!"

FIFTEEN

Starting the Day with Morning Prayer

Invigorated by a good night's sleep and eager to make plans for his mini-break, Tedesco explained to Barker that they were leaving early this morning as they were going to morning prayer before work.

Barker, an amenable soul, followed his master without demur and, once they were safely inside the tranquil Chapel of St Nonna, he fell asleep in front of an old cope chest, designed to store the vestments worn by the priests in centuries past.

Canon Wilfred Drake – at least, according to Tedesco – the saintliest priest remaining in the Church of England, was led into the chapel by one of the vergers.

The congregation numbered about ten and Tedesco was by some way the youngest.

The private detective harboured his moments of doubt but, on balance, he would still describe himself as an Anglican, and this type of service – quiet, still and requiring little or no participation from the worshippers – suited him best. It was his version of mindfulness.

The service was a short one and passed quickly, so before

he knew it, Tedesco was queuing up to be greeted by Canon Wilf as the congregation exited the chapel.

"Good to have you with us, John. And Barker too! Now, I expect you want to see me."

"Am I that transparent, Canon Precentor? Are you free for a quick five minutes once the congregation have left?"

While Wilf chatted to an elderly couple for whom the encounter might be the only one they would have that day, Tedesco and Barker headed for the refectory, which had just opened.

Canon Wilf was soon joining them and Tedesco arranged for a pot of Minster Blend tea to be brought to their table.

Apart from the serving staff, no one else was about yet. The hordes of visitors would start to descend from about 9.30am, so, for now, there was no danger of the two friends being overheard.

Tedesco said, lightly, "I was wondering if there is a date for the Commander's funeral yet?"

Wilfred Drake replied, "I haven't heard anything. I would have thought that his death was due to natural causes or whatever, but I gather that the body hasn't been released yet. Do you know anything about it?"

Tedesco, somewhat sheepishly, told the canon that there was a suggestion that the death might be suspicious but that he couldn't say much more at this stage.

"Anyway," he continued, "Jos is pretty worried about the funeral."

"Of course! His first outing as head sidesman! What a baptism of fire! I expect that the old sea dog will have left instructions for naval ratings to bear his coffin, Marine bands, gun salutes on Cathedral Green…"

"And we can guess what the final hymn will be."

"'For Those in Peril on the Sea'?"

"It's a racing certainty."

"Tell him not to worry. I think the dean will have the harder task: trying to find kind words to say about someone who was a major pain in the cathedral's backside. I will make sure that Jos is the first to know once the date is in the official diary."

"There is another point I wanted to bring up."

"I had rather assumed that there would be."

Tedesco told Wilf about the strangely coincidental deaths of Foster and Verity. He didn't go into detail but explained that as he and Jos had been among the last people to see them alive, the police had asked about their movements on the night in question.

"Wilf, think carefully. Did you see me and Jos walking home together last week? It was Tuesday night."

"It was very cold, as I recall. Let me think. Yes, I did see you. I waved at you, as I remember. But I didn't see Jos. Sorry, I am guessing from your expression that this isn't what you were hoping for."

After a few minutes of idle catching up, Wilf left for a meeting of cathedral chapter while Tedesco and Barker made the short journey to Minster Precincts.

Once Tedesco had caught up with his paperwork, he headed up to see Jos, who was hard at work on his laptop.

He gave him the bad news that Wilf couldn't help with an alibi, but that he would make sure that he had plenty of notice for the funeral.

"Are you still planning this trip to Madeira?"

"Yes, I have texted Nicky and asked her to call, and Sally is looking into flights."

"But won't the police drag me back in? What if I'm charged?"

"Look, you are bound to be anxious, but they will need to come up with more than fingerprints on a bottle. I wouldn't go if I was really worried about you and I will have a word with Paula Fordham before I set off."

Paula was an Exeter-based lawyer, the best criminal defence solicitor in Devon. She has previously featured in several of Tedesco's investigations.

"If you do get called in, contact Paula at once. But I have every confidence that you won't be."

SIXTEEN

Madeira: Introducing Tony Camacho

Scanning the passengers as they staggered through the arrivals lounge managing to appear simultaneously bewildered and agitated after their delayed flight from Gatwick, Tony Camacho felt like a total loser as he held up his laminated sign which read 'Madeiran Magic'.

Was it the whiney-looking couple in the matching Hawaiian shirts? Or could it be the family of misshapen blobs who were peering anxiously at the printout of their travel itinerary?

Third time lucky? It had to be them.

Mr and Mrs Wadhurst from Hayward's Heath. They looked like a Mr and Mrs Wadhurst.

And if they weren't from Hayward's Heath, then they would be from Basingstoke or maybe Bracknell. Or if they weren't from any of these places, then they jolly well should be.

The husband was scuttling about like a demented beetle, while she, by way of contrast, was the physical embodiment of the word 'stolid', probably a leading light in the ladies' bowls team, or the church flower club, so it came as no great surprise to Tony when she marched up to him.

"Are you from Madeiran Magic?"

Nah, I just nicked this sign for a laugh, he thought to himself, but this somehow came out as, "Welcome to Madeira. I'm Tony. Can I assist you with your luggage?"

Having wheeled the matching tartan suitcases to his waiting BMW 3 Series, then checking to make sure that his guests were securely strapped into their seat belts, Tony headed out of the airport towards Funchal.

The Wadhursts were staying at the Quinta da Jinta on a hill just outside the bustling little city, but within walking distance of the centre.

The hotel offered an on-demand courtesy minibus. This had been a decisive factor in the couple's choice of accommodation, as walking back from town could be an issue if Mr Wadhurst's sciatica began to play up.

Once he had driven past the turning for Funchal, Tony put his foot to the floor. No danger of any speed traps out here.

Mr Wadhurst clung tightly to his wife. He whispered, "This chap drives with a certain panache, doesn't he, dear?"

Then, suddenly, they had arrived at the Quinta, and Carlos the superannuated bellboy grinned as he waved Tony through the barrier before the driver brought the car to a screeching halt, kicking up a dust storm on the gravel drive.

Once he had bundled his shell-shocked charges out of the BMW, Tony opened the boot and handed the luggage to Carlos, accepting a twenty-euro tip from his passengers before slyly slipping them his card, which read:

Tony Camacho
Funchal's Gentleman Extraordinaire
At your service, Monday to Friday
Rosalita's Bar from 6pm

*

Tedesco had been on the same flight from Gatwick. The delay had given him plenty of time to question his sanity in deciding on a whim to pursue a private investigation with next to nothing to go on.

However, now that he was airborne, he had better come up with a plan.

Unlike the Wadhursts, he didn't have anyone picking him up on his arrival at the airport, so he waited in line for a taxi.

Sally had booked him into a three-star hotel, near the fish market, called The Scabbard, which he later discovered was the iconic Madeiran fish that lived in the depths off the island's coast. Despite its formidable appearance, it was a regular on the menu at Funchal's best restaurants.

The taxi driver, whose broken English was limited to discussions about football, seemed disappointed that Tedesco didn't support a premier league club. He had, to the bafflement of the Devonian detective, never heard of Plymouth Argyle.

There was no room to park outside the hotel, so Tedesco had to walk about fifty metres in muggy heat, dragging his battered old suitcase behind him.

Once he'd checked in, he showered, lay on the bed and fell into a deep sleep.

SEVENTEEN

Rhyminster: The Investigation Continues

While Tedesco and Barker were concentrating on morning prayers at the cathedral, a very different morning ritual was taking place at the Bristol Road Police Station.

Also referred to as morning prayers, this was a CID catch-up before the day ran away with itself.

Present in the makeshift incident room were DCI Julia Tagg, DS Matt Lovell and DC Jade Sennen.

Matt Lovell soon got Tagg up to speed with Jos Elsted.

"He was very cooperative, and he doesn't seem to have any obvious motive, but there is the fingerprint evidence."

"And he was clear that the bottle we found at Foster's place wasn't one that is commonly used for Madeira," Sennen added.

"Yeah, I can't see cuddly Jos as a serial killer," Tagg said, "if that's what we have, of course, but we need to remember that he and the Commander didn't get on. As Matt will recall, our late bishop was no friend of the LGBT community, nor was Foster."

"And," Matt interjected, "don't forget that Foster was overthrown from his prized role as head sidesman. And who was chosen in his place?"

DC Sennen again: "But wouldn't that give Foster a motive rather than Elsted? Elsted won, so why would he want to kill the man he's defeated?"

"We've already discussed that," said Tagg. "Listen, let's leave Jos on the back burner for now. We need to find out about the prussic acid. Who would have access to it?"

"The two doctors," ventured DS Lovell.

"And what about Mr and Mrs Clayton?" said DC Sennen.

Seeing the blank faces of her senior colleagues, she went on.

"They used to run a garden centre. They'd know about weedkillers and so on."

"Good work. And speaking of noxious substances, I think we need another word with our Mr Smedley."

"Ma'am?" said Lovell, confused.

"The awful stink that accompanies him was present in Foster's room, so it follows that Smedley must have been there. We haven't established how Foster got to the Glug, Glug meeting – could Smedley have picked him up?"

"So," said DCI Tagg, winding up the meeting, "I will speak with the doctors again. Jade, see what you can find out from the Claytons, which leaves you, Matt, with the lovely job of pressing Martin about his movements before the tasting."

DS Lovell looked suitably sick at the prospect.

EIGHTEEN

Madeira: Tedesco Settles In

Waking with a start and still feeling a bit grobbly – a word Tedesco had invented to describe the grimy sensation of having spent a day travelling – he was surprised to notice that it was getting dark. He must have slept for five hours.

Taking the creaky lift down to reception, he asked the helpful receptionist, who spoke flawless English, to recommend somewhere to eat nearby.

Within minutes he was settling down to a delicious fish supper at the imaginatively named Café Funchal.

Once he'd eaten, as he waited for his coffee and his bill, he whipped out his phone and called his home number.

His sister Nicky answered on the second ring.

She said, urgently, "Barker and I were worried stiff! You said you would call when you arrived."

"Don't beat me up, Nicky. I was exhausted when I got to the hotel and so I switched the phone off and had a snooze."

"Where are you now? Enjoying the fleshpots of Funchal no doubt."

"Of course not. I'm just finishing supper, if you must know. Anyway, how is Barker?"

"He's fine. Sally brought him round just after I got in from work and we are getting on like a house on fire, aren't we, Barker?"

"Woof!" he barked.

"And I'm fine as well, thanks for asking," Nicky added.

"Sorry, sorry, I should have asked, and I do appreciate you doing this, but being without Barker just doesn't seem right."

"He will be fine, you soft old thing. I never asked you, what exactly are you up to over there? Is it to do with the Glug, Glug affair?"

In a mildly outraged tone, Tedesco replied, "What! Who have you been talking to? There is no Glug, Glug affair. I am just enjoying a well-deserved mini-break."

"Touchy! Now call me tomorrow – and I hope the investigation goes well."

"Nicky, there is no investigation. Oh blast!" he exclaimed as he realised that his sister had ended the call.

As he made his way back to The Scabbard Hotel, he took a couple of wrong turns, his mind distracted by what Nicky had told him. It sounded like the local media might be starting to sniff around. Someone on the ground had made the connection between Foster and Verity. His money was on Julie 'It Makes Me Mad!' Stringer.

*

He was up bright and early the next morning, and after a pleasant stroll along the waterfront, he ambled through the fish market, captivated by the colourful hustle and bustle and the abundance of the produce. The scabbard fish on display really did look terrifying with their long, thin, jet-black bodies and their sharp piranha-like teeth.

He returned to his hotel for breakfast, which was served al fresco, and then he decided to commence his investigations on the waterfront, where he had noticed various pop-up booths advertising excursions and timeshares.

As he handed in his key at reception, the man on duty asked him about his plans for the day.

"I am looking into some business matters for a client in the UK," he said.

"In that case, my friend, let me give you this," said the guy, handing him a business card.

Tedesco, assuming it was another dining recommendation, was about to shove it in his jacket pocket, but something made him read it.

The card read:

Tony Camacho
Funchal's Gentleman Extraordinaire
At your service, Monday to Friday
Rosalita's Bar from 6pm

"Nothing moves on this island without Mr Tony knowing about it," said the receptionist.

The Devon-based detective retraced his steps from earlier that morning. The pop-up timeshare outlets were open now and he was soon being harangued by a series of determined salespeople.

He decided that it might be worth his while seeking out the all-knowing Tony Camacho before he took any further steps. He was probably a charlatan, but it sounded like he would be the sort of chap who might have an 'in' with the timeshare touts.

He found Rosalita's Bar on a side street not far from where he was staying, so, feeling thirsty, he called in for a lemonade to quench his thirst.

The woman who served him, who may well have been the eponymous Rosalita, was small, dark-haired and of indeterminate age, anywhere from late thirties to mid-fifties was Tedesco's guess.

He showed her Tony Camacho's card and asked if he might be in.

She said, abruptly, in broken English: "You not read?"

"Excuse me?"

"It say from 6pm."

"Of course. So shall I come back at 6pm?"

She shrugged and moved on to her next customer.

Tedesco decided that as he was kind of on holiday, he might as well do some sightseeing, so he took the cable car up to Monte, admiring the views as he ascended to the little hilltop town.

Once there, he bought a prego sandwich from a local bakery, which was as delicious as advertised in the guidebook, and watched with bemused interest as reckless tourists were pushed down the steep hill back to Funchal in wicker carriages known as *carros de cesto*, or basket cars.

He took some photos on his new phone, which he would show Nicky when he got home. He wasn't going to send them. He didn't want the world to know where he was, and he wasn't sure that he even knew how to attach a photo to an email or whatever you did.

As he left the bakery, he was accosted by one of the basket

pushers who assumed that he wanted to hurtle down the hill at speed.

Tedesco tried to explain that one would need to be a basket case to take up such an offer, but this was lost on the man who wandered off, shaking his head.

Having returned by means of the much safer-looking cable car, he decided to take a siesta back at The Scabbard. He'd need his wits about him for the evening.

He'd brought Agatha Christie's *Sparkling Cyanide* with him as holiday reading, having always meant to read it. He'd managed to pick up a rare copy at an antiquarian bookshop in Lyme Regis, with the original Tom Adams cover. This type of detail mattered to him.

For some detectives, crime fiction might be the last thing they wanted to spend their down time with, but Tedesco had always enjoyed a good whodunit.

These days, his tastes veered to the modern exponents of the cosy genre: Elly Griffiths, Richard Osman and so on, but good old Agatha was still his go-to girl.

Having made a solid start to his new book – fifty pages – and enjoyed a decent doze, he felt an extra spring in his step as he set out into the warm evening air.

Arriving at Rosalita's, he was surprised to find that there was already a sizeable queue forming.

The bar was nice enough, but it wasn't the type of place where you expected to queue for a table at 6pm.

Rosalita – he had correctly assumed that the woman who had served him earlier was indeed the proprietor – informed him that if he was here to see Mr Tony, he would have to wait his turn.

She gave Tedesco a cloakroom ticket with a number on

– he was number six – and suggested that he order a drink from the bar and take it to one of the outside tables.

He opted for a glass of Blandy's Madeira – he may as well try the local speciality – and had sampled two more glasses by the time Rosalita arrived with the news that Mr Camacho was free to see him.

He was led into a small office, which reeked of cigar smoke.

Tony Camacho emerged from behind what Tedesco assumed to be a reproduction antique desk and greeted his supplicant warmly.

He was a tall man with a full head of salt-and-pepper hair. He was well built, but somehow not intimidatingly so, well over six feet, and he wore tinted glasses, a black roll-neck and pricey-looking black jeans.

He spoke in a mid-Atlantic drawl which reminded Tedesco of someone.

Later the same evening, as he was about to continue with his book, he realised that it was the chap who used to present *Ski Sunday*, David Vine, who Camacho sounded like.

Introductions duly made, Tedesco gave him one of his own business cards, which Camacho studied closely, then he said, "Mr Tedesco, a fellow private detective. What brings you to our lovely island of Madeira?"

NINETEEN

Meanwhile, Back in Rhyminster

DCI Tagg, normally the poster girl for unflappability, was having her patience sorely tested by the Woolford GP surgery.

Having been treated to interminable music for what seemed like several days, she was eventually able to speak to a human, or at least an approximation of one.

"Are you a patient, madam?" asked the receptionist.

"No, I am a police officer, and I would like to speak to Dr Mark or Dr Susan Elphick."

"Are you registered here?"

Tagg replied, firmly, "No. As I explained, I am a police officer. Please put me through."

"I see. You are not registered here."

Tagg, with growing exasperation, retorted, "Are you going to help me, or will I have to charge you with obstruction?"

The receptionist, flustered now, advised Tagg that she had no right to speak to her like this and that she was going to end the call. Radio silence ensued and then a new voice spoke to the DCI.

"Hello, I am Rosemary Miles, the practice manager. Our receptionist has advised me that she has been spoken to in a disrespectful manner and—"

Tagg interjected, "Did she explain that I am a police officer and that I had politely asked to speak to one of the partners?"

"Er, no, she didn't say that," said Rosemary Miles. "Who am I speaking to?"

"DCI Julia Tagg. Can you find out if either of the doctors are available to speak to me later today?"

"Oh, I see. Yes, of course, DCI Tagg. Leave it with me."

Two hours later, Tagg's deep dive into her admin backlog was interrupted by her loud mobile ringtone, the opening bars of Beyonce's 'Crazy in Love'.

Whenever she heard it, it reminded her that she was still the coolest aunt on the planet.

"DCI Tagg? Sue Elphick from the Woolford Practice. I am really sorry that you were dealt with so inconsiderately this morning."

Tagg replied, "I quite understand. I am sure that NHS receptionists are under way too much pressure these days."

"That is so understanding of you," said Sue Elphick. "Look, if you need to call me again, why don't you text me on this number? Now, how can I help? I assume it is to do with what we talked about the other day?"

"It is, and this is highly confidential."

The DCI could almost feel Dr Sue looking serious and nodding her agreement down the line.

Tagg went on, "We now know that both Commander Foster and Verity Glynde were the victims of poisoning. I have to ask, does the practice have any access to, for example, cyanide?"

Dr Sue thought carefully before responding.

"I know that a form of it is used in clinical treatment as a follow-up with diabetic patients, to monitor ketones in their urine, and have heard of it being used in emergency medicine to rapidly reduce blood pressure but no, a GP practice like ours wouldn't often have need of it."

"But could you access it?"

"In theory, maybe…"

"Dr Sue, that has been most helpful. And again, please keep this to yourself. We are at an early stage of the investigation and so we are looking at a wide range of possibilities."

"Of course, of course. Mark and I are at your disposal, anything we can do."

"I will bear that in mind. Sorry for interrupting your busy day."

While her boss was quizzing Dr Sue, DC Jade Sennen was enjoying tea and cake in Jim and Mary Clayton's conservatory overlooking their immaculate garden.

The retired couple seemed quite excited at having a second CID operative calling on them and were only too eager to speculate, unbidden, about who might be behind the unexplained deaths of their fellow gluggers.

"I hope you are interviewing that awful man Greville Jackson," said Jim. "He's a rum bugger, if you ask me."

Mary jumped in. "Jim! Don't use language like that!"

"I'm sure you've heard much worse, haven't you, lass?" said Jim.

"Oh, tons worse!" Sennen replied, although she could do without being referred to as a lass, she thought to herself.

"I must agree with my husband though," said Mary.

"Greville Jackson always had it in for the Commander," Jim said. "Chalk and cheese, you see. Military man and a theatrical."

Mary added, "And Greville was horrid to poor Verity, wasn't he, Jim?"

Jim agreed. "Aye, he was always rude to her when she gave out her marks for the wines. I wish I'd done more to defend her, but she was quite good at standing up to him, to be fair," he reflected.

Jade Sennen decided to put a stop to the speculation.

"We are speaking to anyone who knew the deceased, and that includes the members of Glug, Glug."

"That's good to hear, but make sure to give Jackson priority," Jim said.

Jade, trying not to sound impatient, said, "Now, you are probably wondering why I am here this morning. I need to ask you about your time in the garden centre."

Mary uncrossed her legs and leant forward. "How can we help?" she said.

"While you were working, did you ever use or supply any products that might have contained prussic acid?"

Jim puffed his cheeks out and then exhaled loudly before replying, "I think it might be used in some weedkillers, but it's dangerous stuff."

"Didn't Peter LaGarde ask you about weedkillers?" Mary asked him.

"He did and all. He's got a huge garden, you see, and his gardener was flummoxed by an outbreak of hogweed. Peter asked me about it after one of the wine tastings, not the latest one, maybe the one before."

Jade pushed him. "And did you offer any advice?"

"I mentioned a product called 'Weed Murderer'. It isn't available to the public. You can order it through a garden centre, but they will carry out checks before they agree to get hold of it."

"And I suppose you might be able to get it from some dodgy website these days," Mary added.

"Right then, Mr and Mrs Clayton," said Jade. "That is all for now. You have been most helpful. And thank you for the delicious cake."

While Mary went to fetch a jar of chutney for their visitor, Jim whispered conspiratorially to Jade.

"Do you think he poisoned them with weedkiller then? Jackson?"

*

"This is becoming a tiresomely regular occurrence," said Martin Smedley as he sat down with DS Matt Lovell in the cathedral refectory where they had arranged to meet, as it coincided with the archivist's mid-morning coffee break.

"We are carrying out an important investigation into two suspicious deaths, sir, so we do need to find out as much as we can about Commander Foster and Verity Glynde, which is why we are speaking to their friends."

As Lovell sipped his decaffeinated coffee, he became aware, as he looked around the refectory, of various people pulling faces or holding their noses.

Smedley said, nervously, "I wouldn't describe either of them as friends, Officer."

"Really?" said Lovell, chancing his arm. "But we have reason to think that you visited the late Commander Foster at his house."

Martin Smedley responded tetchily. "I have been there, yes," he said. "We got on reasonably well because we were both heavily involved in the cathedral."

"OK, but why would you visit him at home?" asked Lovell.

"How do you know that I did?" Smedley answered.

Lovell said, as diplomatically as he could manage, "You have a distinctive musk, sir, which was present at the late Commander's house."

"It is a medical condition! How many times do I have to explain!"

The couple at the next table moved away.

"I am sorry to hear that, but I would still like to know why you visited him at home. You must have seen plenty of each other here at the cathedral."

"I used to give him a lift sometimes."

"Would that include to the wine tastings?"

"Yes."

"I see. Would you give him a lift home as well?"

"No, because whereas his place is on the way to Woolford from the cathedral, it isn't on my way home. He's happy to take a taxi."

"And did you give him a lift the other evening?"

"Funnily enough, no, I wasn't needed. Dr Susan had already offered to take him."

TWENTY

Tedesco Forges an Alliance

Back in Funchal, Tedesco was going through the reasons behind his visit to the lovely island of Madeira.

Camacho, clearly intrigued by what he was hearing, offered his guest a cigar (which the well-mannered Devonian declined gracefully), then he asked to be excused for a minute.

Upon his return, he explained that he had asked Rosalita to send away the other people who were seeking his advice as he wanted to concentrate on Tedesco's developing narrative.

Camacho blew out a geometrically perfect circle of cigar smoke and said, "So, we have two deaths among the members of this wine circle or whatever, and opened bottles of our famous local speciality were found beside the bodies."

Leaning forward, he added, "But you wouldn't come all this way if that was all you had to go on – just the fact that the bottles bore the name of the island, I mean."

Tedesco hesitated.

"Mr Camacho, the situation is very delicate. Before I go further—"

Tony, smiling, interrupted, "You want to know about me. My bona fides. Can I even trust this guy?"

Tedesco, disarmed, nodded in eager agreement.

Camacho explained that he was Madeiran on his father's side, but his mother was from Portsmouth.

Tedesco's face lit up. He said, "I thought I recognised the team photo in the bar. Pompey, Cup Final, 2008."

Camacho smiled. "I didn't have you down as a lover of the beautiful game. Who do you support?"

Swelling with pride, Tedesco proclaimed his lifetime of loyalty to Plymouth Argyle.

"The Janners! Pompey's dockyard rivals," said Camacho, adding that he didn't mind Argyle. He even had a bit of a soft spot for them. It was Southampton that he instinctively disliked.

Over the course of the evening, which carried on into the bar where Rosalita served up the house special, baked scabbard fish, Tedesco learnt that Camacho's parents had met when his mother had a summer job in a hotel on the island and that he had been born and brought up in Funchal.

However, he had spent some time in the UK, studying oceanography at the University of Southampton, where he kept his ancestral Portsmouth connections to himself.

Post-graduation, he enjoyed an itinerant few years spent variously crewing yachts, teaching English as a foreign language and running a beach bar in Cyprus before he settled back in Funchal, where he set himself up as a private investigator.

"I've always been – what would you say – nosey. And I know this island like the back of my hand."

Camacho had ordered a white rioja to accompany the fish.

Tedesco asked him if he drank Madeira.

Camacho, laughing, said, "It tastes like cough medicine. It was invented for you lot, the Brits. Anyway, back to your investigation."

For whatever reason, Tedesco's gut instinct was to trust this man, so he opened up about the timeshare angle.

Camacho, after pausing to ask Rosalita for a fresh carafe of white wine, intimated that this was an area where he felt he could help.

"There are legitimate timeshare firms here, but we also have some – how to put it nicely – cowboys."

He took another drag on his cigar and then added, "I think I can see where you are coming from. One of the members of Glug, Glug – have I got the name right? – has been strong-arming some of the other members into investing in property over here and so you have a second connection to the island. First, the bottles of Madeira and then the timeshare."

"Indeed, you put it most succinctly."

Camacho peered over his shaded glasses momentarily, and then he said, "I have someone I would like you to meet. Why don't we reconvene for breakfast at The Scabbard tomorrow, say 9.30am?"

"How do you know where I am staying?" asked Tedesco.

"I know everything that happens in Funchal, Mr Tedesco."

As he weaved his way back to the hotel along the now-familiar route, John Tedesco sent texts firstly to Jos Elsted, asking how things were going, and then to his sister Nicky, asking after Barker.

Once he was back in his room, he googled 'Glug, Glug' and, after scrolling through various dodgy websites, he found the site for the wine society.

The social-media-averse detective hadn't realised that Glug, Glug even had a web presence, but he was delighted to find that it contained pictures of the members enjoying themselves at various tastings and trips to English vineyards. This would be most useful.

Just as he was about to resume his Agatha Christie, his phone pinged. It was Jos.

The funeral for Commander Foster would be taking place in the quire of Rhyminster Cathedral in five days' time.

*

Tedesco was awake early. He had tried to delay his emergence into the day by continuing with *Sparkling Cyanide*, but was too intrigued by Tony Camacho and his mystery man to be able to give his full attention to the plot, so he went for a stroll around the block before breakfast.

He was growing to like Funchal and momentarily allowed himself the conceit of imagining himself returning there one day with the woman of his dreams.

A now-familiar voice, the mid-Atlantic tones of Tony Camacho, snapped him out of his reverie.

"Mr Tedesco! A man who likes an early morning perambulation. I always start the day like this, helps to clear the head."

Walking back to The Scabbard with his new friend, Tedesco was struck by how often various shopkeepers and stall holders emerged to greet Camacho, either to tell him about their latest woes or just to shout, 'Hey, Big Man' or something similar as the 'gentleman extraordinaire' made his daily *passeggiata*.

Tedesco also noted that his new pal was, once again, dressed in black, but that he had replaced the roll-neck of the previous evening with a Hugo Boss polo shirt.

It was gone 9.30am by the time they reached Tedesco's hotel.

The desk guy rushed to greet Camacho, shaking his hand with great vigour before he looked at Tedesco and said, "So you have met Tony! He is a great guy. How do you say – a legend!"

The waiting staff were equally excited to see who had joined Tedesco for breakfast and they all wanted to share their latest news with Mr Tony, so it was a good hour before the two of them were able to set off for the famous Reid's Hotel.

It was about two kilometres away, a steep climb, so Camacho called a cab, which arrived almost immediately.

The cabbie made a fuss of 'Mr Tony', which Tedesco now realised was the norm, but the man in black was able to momentarily interrupt the driver's monologue to tell his fellow private eye that he had arranged to meet the mystery man at 11am, so they should be bang on time.

Upon arrival at Reid's, the two of them were swept into the immaculate reception area where they were greeted by a short, red-faced, tubby man, who looked as if he had spent a lifetime loitering in the lobbies of luxury hotels.

Camacho strode towards the little fellow, who stood up to greet him and then he made the introductions.

"John Tedesco, this is Reggie Challenor."

Tedesco took in the personage in front of him. Where had he seen him before?

Of course! Whenever the latest royal scandal broke and a talking head was required, you would find Sir Reginald Challenor.

He had been a regular on daytime TV sofas ever since the fallout from Diana. What had he been? An equerry maybe, a private secretary to some random minor royal, or perhaps he held an ancient title, like First Spoon-Licker Pursuivant or some such.

Tedesco followed behind at a slight distance as Sir Reginald led them to a small outside table nestled into a belvedere which offered stunning views over the Atlantic coast in both directions.

"We should be safe here," Sir Reginald drawled.

"Now, Mr Lupescu," he went on, "Tony tells me that you are here on business." He paused for effect, and then he said, with relish, "Deaths in suspicious circumstances, eh?"

Tedesco paused to consider whether to put Sir Reginald right about his surname, decided that it would appear chippy and replied, "Sir Reginald, it's a great pleasure to meet you. Just to explain my background. I was a solicitor for many years—"

"A lawyer, eh?" said the royal expert, disapprovingly.

Tedesco, ignoring the barb, continued, "And now I am a private investigator based in Rhyminster. I also have an interest in a small wine-importing business."

Sir Reginald jumped back in.

"Rhyminster, you say? All that trouble with the last bishop?"

"Indeed, but we are putting that behind us. I am here in Madeira because there have been two recent deaths in my home city. Both the deceased persons were members of the same wine appreciation society."

"And," Camacho interjected, "both were found dead beside a doctored bottle of our local wine."

"I say," said Sir Reginald. "So there might be a connection to the island?"

Tedesco, wisely resisting the temptation to say, 'No shit, Sherlock', opted instead to explain to the ruddy-faced aristocrat that there was a second possible link to the island: the lucrative market in selling timeshares to gullible tourists, particularly those with UK passports.

Sir Reginald's rather prominent ears visibly pricked up at the mention of timeshares.

"Timeshare touts – blackguards, the lot of them! My nephew Bertie, the silly ass, got himself tied up in knots by some unsavoury coves who recruited him to flog the bally things.

"Tony here knows everyone on the island, and thanks to his good offices we were able to get Bertie – he really is a prize nincompoop – safely out of harm's way. I still had to buy off these crooks though!"

"I am sorry to hear that, Sir Reginald. I'm afraid that these people, or people like them, have been applying strong-arm tactics to try and convince members of the wine society – it's called Glug, Glug, by the way – to make investments in timeshares here in Funchal."

"Glug, Glug, you say? Frightfully good name, what!" said Sir Reginald, adding that he would be pleased to help in any way that he could.

Tedesco somewhat inelegantly reached for his phone and showed the photos from the Glug, Glug website to each of his companions in turn.

"What do you reckon, Tony? It's him!" said Sir Reginald.

Tedesco looked across at Camacho, who stared intently at the image on the small screen, which was of a Glug, Glug trip to a vineyard in Sussex.

"Reggie, I think you are right. It's Charlie Fairfax."

He handed the phone back to Tedesco and indicated Fairfax to him.

He was pointing at a decidedly squiffy-looking Peter LaGarde.

TWENTY-ONE

The Boring Couple Just Got Interesting

There was a palpable element of tension in the air at 26 Crosshill Drive, Derrington, the nondescript home of the nondescript couple Stephen and Rachel Lowndes.

Thunderbirds One and Two were still in the drive awaiting take off; in his case, to the nearby primary school, and in hers, to the architects' practice, which was in a barn conversion just outside Woolford.

"Look, darling, what is it? You haven't touched your bircher muesli again, and you disappeared to the spare room last night. Don't think I didn't hear you creeping back in."

Rachel considered her reply before responding carefully but firmly that the practice should never have accepted their latest commission. The client was a nightmare, forever changing his instructions and then questioning the revised estimates for his latest hare-brained idea. She couldn't get to sleep for worrying about it.

"You never normally bring your work home. If I ask you about it, you just shut off."

"I'm not a robot, you know! I do have feelings!"

"You didn't show any when poor Verity died. I couldn't believe how cold you were."

Rachel stood up.

"I need to get to the office. I'm seeing a prospective new client at 9am, not that you would be in the least bit interested."

As she picked up the keys to Thunderbird Two, she looked over her shoulder and by way of a parting salvo she calmly addressed her husband: "Why would you expect me to react with anything other than cool indifference to the news that my husband's mistress has been found dead?"

TWENTY-TWO

Madeira Again

After a long, languid and liquid lunch with Sir Reginald, Tony texted the cabbie to drop Tedesco back at The Scabbard.

The old royal expert had been in his element, regaling his audience with evermore outrageous anecdotes, some comic, some salacious and several of them comprising elements of both.

Tedesco was, however, able to return with one pearl of information from Sir Reggie before the conversation turned to the antics of various minor European royals, of whom he had barely heard.

Among the photos on the Glug, Glug website was one that had intrigued the by-now-pickled aristocrat.

"It's good old Spraggers!" he roared, looking at a picture of Sylvia Spraggon taken on one of the club's outings to a winery near Rheims in which she was pictured standing next to an outsize champagne bottle with her mouth firmly affixed to the nozzle.

"She taught our daughters! They hated her, but Clara and I thought she was wonderful! She should be running the country!"

Tedesco was momentarily struck dumb by a vision of

Sylvia in number 10 Downing Street offering a choice of builder's or lesbo tea to the visiting US President.

It turned out that Tony Camacho had also recognised the retired headmistress, as she had consulted him about aggressive sales tactics from the timeshare thugs.

Now, thought Tedesco, *Sylvia has spoken about visiting Madeira and hasn't she also mentioned Peter LaGarde – or was he in fact Charlie Fairfax – in the context of timeshares?*

Once he was back in his hotel room, the Devonian detective fell into a deep sleep, then woke up with a start, realising that it was evening.

Deciding that he was still sated by the huge lunch, he went down to the bar and sat down with a glass of Blandy's Madeira – he was beginning to develop a taste for it – and his precious Agatha Christie.

Returning to his book, he was struck by two new things: a reference to cyanide being kept by most gardeners, or words to that effect, and the fact that it tended to be used in crystalline form.

The lovely Lancastrian couple, Jim and Mary, had been gardeners of course. He expected that DCI Julia Tagg, no one's idea of a fool, might have made that connection.

But how about Rachel Lowndes? She was an architect.

Her practice was well known locally for designing the modern equivalent of stately homes – which Jos rudely referred to as footballers' palaces – and they usually came complete with landscaped gardens.

So might Rachel and her partners employ their own landscape gardeners, or else contract with a gardening firm? And might such a firm have access to potassium cyanide in crystal form?

As he ordered a second glass of Blandy's Duke of Clarence, he reflected that his little trip had yielded some clues which he could take back to Rhyminster.

He had learnt about the high-pressure timeshare salesmen from Tony, who had recognised Peter LaGarde, as had Sir Reggie – but they both knew him as Charlie Fairfax, which was, to put it mildly, interesting.

Sylvia Spraggon had consulted Tony about the timeshare tactics, so it would be worth crossing the road to quiz his irascible neighbour upon his return home even if it meant sharing a glass or two of the Stonker with her.

If LaGarde/Fairfax had been among those who had menaced her in Funchal then Sylvia would have had a motive for nudging the investigation towards the Madeiran angle.

And Pete himself – just who was he, and who was Poppy, and just how did they accumulate so much wealth, with no apparent effort?

He'd discussed the poisoning aspect with his new friend 'Mr Tony', who was intrigued by the insertion of the cyanide into the bottles of Madeira.

He thought that the poison might have discoloured the wine, which should have put the drinker on notice that something was up.

"And what about the taste?" Tedesco had asked him.

"It might have improved it," Camacho had replied.

Tedesco would need to develop the 'crystals' theory that he had picked up from his book.

Good old Agatha, he thought. *Two Devon-based detectives working together at last!*

And as he turned in for the night, he wondered whether

he should print some business cards like those used by his new friend.

John Tedesco
Rhyminster's shy detective
Strictly by appointment only
Clients must be dog-friendly

Maybe not his best idea…

TWENTY-THREE

A Gift-Wrapped Clue

DS Matt Lovell hung around uncertainly, unsure when to interrupt DCI Julia Tagg, who was engrossed with something on her police computer.

She looked up suddenly and said, "Matt. Never had you down as the hovering type. I assume it's important?"

"It could be. Jade Sennen has been going through the SOCO report from Verity Glynde's place in the Cathedral Close."

"And?"

"They discovered a gift bag – you know, the ones that are designed to fit a wine bottle."

Tagg nodded.

"Anyway," Lovell went on, "there was a gift tag attached to it."

"Was there a message?"

"There was. It said, 'All my love, Steve.'"

"I see. So the obvious inference is that the gift bag contained the bottle of Madeira. Any prints on it?"

"That's the interesting thing. Verity clearly handled the bag and the card, but there is another set of prints which are only visible on the card."

Julia Tagg stood up and paced for thirty seconds.

"OK. So who might Steve be?"

"I've been thinking about that. If this is linked to Glug, Glug – which is our working hypothesis – then the only member of the group who it might be is…"

Tagg cut in.

"Stephen Lowndes. He doesn't strike me as a natural 'Steve' exactly, but we need to get him in. Send DC Sennen along to his primary school when it closes for the day. We just need a set of prints at this stage. I wouldn't expect any trouble from him."

"Will do. Oh, there was a message from our friend Tedesco. He's been away and says that he has some ideas he wants to kick about with you."

Tagg smiled. "I'm sure he does. Nicky let slip that he's been in Madeira."

*

On the surface, Stephen Lowndes had been only too happy to cooperate with the police, but when Rachel arrived home that evening, she found her normally docile husband boiling with pent-up frustration.

"Why are you always so bloody late? I've been home for ages. As usual!"

"How many times? Being a partner is not a nine-to-five job," said Rachel, glacially.

"Unlike teaching infants, I suppose. Oh yeah, no pressure at all."

"Just grow up. At least your job gives you plenty of opportunity to play away."

"I knew it! You couldn't wait to bring that up, could you? Anyway, I wasn't home on time today as I was dragged into the police station to have my fingerprints done."

Trying not to look too smug, let alone pleased, Rachel reassured him that the police would be taking prints from all the gluggers.

"I expect that it will be me next," she said, failing to suppress a smirk.

TWENTY-FOUR

The Wanderer Returns

Tony Camacho had insisted on driving Tedesco to the airport, despite the fact that it was an early morning departure.

"When's your flight? I'll pick you up an hour before it leaves."

"But it clearly states that I need to be at the check-in at least two hours beforehand."

Mr Tony laughed. "I can park right outside departures. I'll let the airport know that you have been in Madeira to see me and they will do the rest."

"Fast-track me, as it were."

"If you like."

After a white-knuckle ride to the airport in Tony's limo, they were greeted on arrival by a member of the airport staff, who scooted Tedesco to the head of the check-in queue, whisked him through VIP security and then handed him to a uniformed driver who drove him onto the tarmac, where he was met by an air hostess who led him to the best seat on the plane.

As he settled down with a glass of champagne, Tedesco reflected that his new friend was indeed a 'gentleman extraordinaire'.

The flight was on time, but as soon as he landed at Gatwick the familiar problems started – long wait at passport control, even longer wait at the luggage carousel, non-functioning barrier at the off-site car park, lanes closed on the M25 – which meant that he didn't arrive home until the early evening.

His sister, stalwart local TV reporter Nicky, was presenting *Searchlight Today* from the studio in Plymouth, so it was a slightly startled Sally, his PA, who greeted him when he arrived back at St Budeaux Place, looking and feeling beyond grobbly.

"Mr T!" she trilled. "Barker and I were getting worried. Nicky was expecting you hours ago so I stepped in."

After bending down to stroke Barker, who welcomed him back with some suitably enthusiastic tail wagging, he thanked Sally, adding that he hoped that she hadn't been inconvenienced.

"I've had to miss morris dancing, but this was an emergency. Barker comes first!"

"Indeed he does, Sally. Look, I'm so sorry about the morris dancing. I suppose you have literally let the side down."

Getting no reaction, he asked if she would like to stay for supper.

"Oh no, that's alright. I will cycle home now. I've got some tofu and noodles to use up, so I'll be fine."

After seeing Sally safely to her bicycle, he returned to Barker, gave the border terrier a brief update on his activities, found a Charlie Bigham's fish pie in the freezer – he always kept one for emergencies – and started to warm the oven.

Then he poured himself a large glass of Bordeaux and texted Nicky to call him when she got home.

By the time she called, he had wolfed down the fish pie, luxuriated in a hot bath while listening to Nick Drake and was sitting up in bed trying to finish *Sparkling Cyanide*.

*

Suitably refreshed, he woke the next morning feeling like a man on a mission.

There would be some changes made, oh yes. Tony Camacho had taught him so much during their brief acquaintance.

A puzzled Barker, sensing his master's sudden boost in energy levels, and hoping that this was just a passing phase, followed the detective on their familiar walk to work.

Tedesco was greeting everyone he met with an unusual vigour, which prompted his friend Canon Wilfred to ask him if he was quite alright.

"Never better, Wilf. Let's catch up soon."

The kindly canon wandered towards the cathedral, shaking his head in puzzlement.

Spotting Jos Elsted arriving at the office, he shook him firmly by the hand and asked him how he was.

To his immense disappointment, Jos didn't reply by saying, 'Great to have you back, Big Man', but instead started to talk shop.

Barker looked up at his master as if to say, 'Don't worry, you'll always be the big guy to me'.

As it was going to take a while before his friends cottoned on to his new 'Tony' persona, Tedesco decided to greet Sally in his normal neutral tone, then he got back behind his desk and tried to call Julia Tagg. He got Jade Sennen, who promised to let her boss know that he wanted to see her.

Having caught up with his paperwork, he and Barker set off for their familiar walk to Jenks Bakery, where Tedesco habitually bought his lunch.

He had forgotten that his return to Rhyminster had coincided with the ghastly 'Rhyminster Hat Fest'.

Just why his beloved city had decided about twenty years ago to provide a home for this annual celebration of street theatre was completely beyond him.

Tedesco hated Hat Fest with a passion. Prat Fest, more like. Over-privileged, entitled youths interrupting his lunch break with their moronic mime, magic tricks and audience participation. Why can't they get proper jobs?

Approaching Jenks, he was assailed by an idiot wearing a top hat who asked him if he was interested in joining a flash mob.

Resisting the temptation to say that he would be interested in rounding up a posse designed to drive this berk and his ilk out of town, he walked on and entered his favourite bakery.

"Where have you two been?" asked Joan, who had been serving the detective with his daily baked goods for several decades.

She didn't address him as Big Man either, he noted.

After his lunch al desko, Tedesco updated his case file on the Glug, Glug murders in his immaculate copperplate handwriting until he was interrupted by a call from Julia Tagg.

She could see him at 5pm and was happy to come over. She ended the conversation by asking if Barker would be present. She was another avid fan.

Meanwhile, two other members of Glug, Glug were arriving back in the country.

Peter and Poppy LaGarde, their tans suitably topped up, had flown back from the Bahamas, their journey home eased by their chauffeur-driven Mercedes.

TWENTY-FIVE

Update

"So," Julia Tagg kicked off in her customary breezy tone, "how was Madeira?"

Tedesco gulped.

"How did you know I was there?" he asked. "Hang on. I expect my sister told you."

"Come off it, John. You knew she would. And I assume this little trip had something to do with the wine club?"

"Of course it did. Look, I'm really worried that Jos is getting dragged into this. There is no way that he was involved, even though his labels were affixed to the bottles."

Tagg politely interrupted his flow. She said, "Listen, I get it. And I have an open mind at the moment. But if you have something to share with me, then I'm all ears."

Tedesco's somewhat refined detective agency had worked well with the local force over the cathedral murders, providing crucial evidence, and so Tagg was sensible enough to recognise the value of his input into this more secular mystery.

Tedesco replied, "One of the members of the wine society – they call each other 'gluggers' – told me that she had visited the island and had been targeted by unscrupulous timeshare salesmen."

"Go on."

"Anyway, by a sheer stroke of luck, I met an extraordinary fellow who runs a detective agency in Funchal, and when I mentioned timeshares, he offered to help me.

"And, to cut a very long story short, he introduced me to an expat – a sozzled old royal correspondent – who identified none other than Peter LaGarde as one of the touts."

Tagg appeared to be gripped by the narrative, so Tedesco continued with it.

"And here's the interesting thing. Our friend Pete was going under a different name back then – Charlie Fairfax."

"Was he now? I always thought there was something fishy about him. And I wonder which one of the gluggers he was pushing his timeshares at?"

"It was Sylvia Spraggon. And I have evidence that she was in Madeira at a party with LaGrande, or Fairfax, Carruthers or whoever he really is."

"Fascinating," said Tagg, who silently chose not to let her friend know, at least at this stage, about the possible development in the Verity Glynde case.

And Tedesco silently opted not to tell DCI Tagg that he was going to call in on Sylvia on his way home.

*

Deciding that it would be most unsporting to inflict Sylvia on the long-suffering Barker, he let the border terrier in and fed him supper before crossing the road to catch up with his ebullient neighbour.

"Oh, you decided to come back then! Tell me about Madeira."

Nicky must have blabbed when she was dog sitting.

"Care to join me for a swift Stonker?" Sylvia asked, clearly not prepared to take no for an answer. "Really liked your sister, by the way. I've asked her to join us."

"Us? Oh, you mean the gluggers!" said her guest, somewhat uncertainly.

"Who did you think I meant, man, The Flat Earth Society? Anyway, shoot. What have you found out about the timeshare merchants? Any link with the murders?"

"Sylvia," said Tedesco, in a tone that suggested that he knew that he was taking his life in his hands, "I have a couple of questions for you."

"Well! Get on with it!"

"You have been to Madeira, haven't you?"

"You know I have. Hurry up, will you. *Only Connect* starts in ten minutes."

"Sylvia, did you meet Peter LaGarde when you were there?"

"Don't think so."

"OK. How about Charlie Fairfax?"

"Rings a bell. What has this got to do with the price of chutney?"

"Because Fairfax and LaGarde are one and the same. Look at this."

He showed her his phone and the image that Sir Reginald had shared with him in the gardens of Reid's Hotel.

"It is the awful Pete! Why didn't I recognise him when he moved to Rhyminster?"

"It was a good few years ago," said Tedesco, kindly. "And his hair was dyed blond in those days. Have another look."

"Gordon Bennett! You are not wrong. So it must have been him then. The murderer. LaGarde."

"I think you may be jumping to conclusions, Sylvia."

"And you need to leave before *Only Connect*. Only decent quiz on the box."

TWENTY-SIX

Requiem for a Naval Hero

The cathedral was not completely rammed for Commander Foster's funeral, but it was respectably full for a man of his age, many of whose shipmates would have long predeceased him, their ashes scattered in Davy Jones's locker.

Foster had left detailed instructions concerning the ceremony with his nephew, who had been appointed as his sole executor, a literally thankless task.

His last wishes included the presence of the Band of the Royal Marines, who would lead the coffin into the nave with the stirring march 'Semper Fidelis', not only the Marines' anthem but also that of Tedesco's beloved Plymouth Argyle Football Club.

The Marines politely declined the invitation as they were busy elsewhere, and because Foster hadn't actually served in the corps.

So it was the band of the local sea scouts that accompanied the coffin, the sheer weight of which was proving a challenge even for the experienced pall-bearers used by I.J Clemo and Sons, Foster's choice of undertaker.

The selection of the anthem still rankled with Tedesco,

as Foster hated football and had spent most of his career onshore, so posing as a man with Royal Marine connections was another red flag for the gentle detective, who was himself the son of a decorated chief petty officer.

Chief sidesman Jos Elsted had managed to blag his friend John a prime seat in the quire, from where Tedesco idly mused on the choice of music for his own funeral.

As Foster had sullied 'Semper Fidelis' for him, then he would have 'He Who Would Valiant Be', with its chorus 'To Be a Pilgrim' – Argyle were known as 'The Pilgrims' – or he might consider Argyle's unofficial anthem, 'The Janner Song'.

He smiled to himself at the thought of the stuffy Rhyminster congregation singing along to that one.

There were a number of uniformed officers in the front row of the nave, and one of them, who bore an uncanny resemblance to the deceased, marched forward purposefully to read the first lesson. He turned out to be Foster's unfortunate nephew.

The reading was from Psalm 107: "Those who go down to the sea in ships and ply their trade in great waters, these have seen the works of the Lord and his wonders in the deep."

It was beautifully read, and Tedesco belatedly wished that he had chosen it for his own father.

A god-daughter gave a perfectly delivered reading of Tennyson's *Crossing the Bar*, which Tedesco had read at his father's funeral at St Andrew's church in Plymouth.

After the cathedral choir led the congregation in a stirring rendition of 'For Those in Peril on the Sea', the stage was set for the address, which was to be delivered by Canon Wilfred Drake.

As well as his responsibility for music and liturgy at the

cathedral, Canon Wilf was responsible for liaison with the large volunteer community and so he had drawn the short straw of trying to find nice things to say about someone who had been regarded as rude and dismissive to clergy, brusque and unhelpful to visitors, a terrible ambassador for the cathedral and whose lasting legacy was to get poisoned and thence cause gossip and conspiracy theories to abound as to the identity of the murderer.

Tedesco sent up a silent prayer for Wilf to get through the ordeal unscathed.

Canon Wilfred ascended to the pulpit in his usual urgent style, paused to survey the congregation and then made his introductory remarks.

"Thomas Foster, known to most of us as 'the Commander', was not an easy man."

He was relieved to see that many in the congregation were smiling at him, and there were even some audible 'hear, hears'.

"However, Thomas was an incredibly loyal servant of this place and, although his style may have verged on the dictatorial, he kept his fellow sidesmen in order and was a great mentor to countless recruits who joined the volunteer ranks over the years.

"His views were, to many, outdated. But he was a product, as we all are, of his particular times, and while he couldn't reconcile himself to the idea of an openly gay man succeeding him in his role, Jos has told me that Thomas never bore him any personal animosity.

"One of the privileges of this vocation is the chance to meet the relatives of the deceased. Although Thomas didn't have a family of his own, I have learnt from his nephew

Horatio that he was a wonderful uncle, who taught him to sail and who inspired his own decision to serve his country.

"I can, in turn, recall many conversations with Thomas when he expressed his pride in Horatio's stellar progress, and Emma, who gave us that wonderful reading from Tennyson, told me that Thomas was a dutiful godfather, who never forgot birthdays or Christmas."

Then it came to the hard part of the address, which Wilf decided to attack head-on.

"Why anyone would wish to end the life of this faithful servant, we may never know. I would, however, ask you all to pray for the police and all those concerned with investigating this terrible crime to exercise wisdom, diligence and care throughout this difficult time and to pray that truth and justice will prevail."

There was a wake in the cathedral refectory immediately after the service and Tedesco, falling into step with Lady Fiona Derrington, his favourite local aristocrat, commented on how well the service had gone, particularly as social media had finally woken up to the fact that there had been two deaths in quick order.

"I agree, John. The Commander was not to everyone's taste, but Wilf managed to say some positive things."

"Speaking of the media, Fiona—"

A human whirlwind wrapped in a large black shawl suddenly appeared.

It was Julie Stringer of the *Rhyminster Journal*.

TWENTY-SEVEN

The Wake

"Lady Fiona! And John! Two of my favourite people!" said Julie Stringer, oozing and gushing as only she could.

"Nice to see you too, Julie," Tedesco said. "And if you want to discuss recent events, it's a 'no comment' from me," he swiftly added.

"Nor from me, I'm afraid," said Lady Derrington. "I thought it was a super address from Canon Wilfred."

Correctly assessing that she would glean no morsels of gossip from these two, Julie Stringer exited the stage in pursuit of one of the men in uniform.

"She's a piece of work!" said Tedesco.

"She certainly seems to admire our brave sailors," twinkled Lady Fiona, Tedesco resisting the temptation to add 'she goes overboard so easily'.

Looking around, the detective became aware of the oncoming approach of one of the gluggers. Greville Jackson was wandering over, seemingly attracted to Lady Fiona like an iron filing to a magnet as the only other person in the room who remotely matched his social standing.

"Fiona! It's been too long!" he said, bowing theatrically, completely ignoring Tedesco.

"Have you noticed the terrible stink over there? I couldn't avoid Smedley on my way in, so I asked him what he knew about recent events, and he told me that he didn't use the internet and had never owned a television. I replied – rather wittily, I thought – by saying that he may not own a television, but he knew about smell-o-vision!"

"Frightfully amusing," said Her Ladyship, clearly without meaning it.

Tedesco had heard enough, so he politely excused himself and went to find Canon Wilfred to congratulate him on the service.

Wilf was chatting with Jos Elsted, who had provided the wine and was showing all the usual signs of having knocked back a glass or two himself, presumably in relief at having got through the ordeal of the Commander's funeral unscathed.

"He wasn't such a bad fellow, you know," said Jos, squiffily.

Jim and Mary Clayton, who had been hovering shyly on the edge of the conversation, seconded Jos's comment.

"Aye, his bark was worse than his bite," said Jim.

"But he was something of an acquired taste," said Mary.

Canon Wilfred introduced himself to the horticultural duo. Jim instantly stated that they were not regular churchgoers, but Wilf Drake was the master of putting people at ease in the formal cathedral setting and they were soon chatting away like old friends.

The gluggers were gathering now. Jos was greeted by the Drs Elphick, who congratulated him on his choice of wine for the wake.

"I'm guessing, let me see, Zinfandel?" asked Dr Sue.

"Maybe. But where do you think it's from?" teased Jos.

Dr Mark, deep in thought, stated that California would be too obvious, so could it be Italian perhaps?

"Spot on! It's an Italian Primitivo, the terroir is a Mandurian black soil, and they call it 'Zinfandel Californiano' over there."

"Fascinating," said the doctors in unison.

Tedesco made his apologies. He was an enthusiastic wine drinker, but this kind of discussion was way too hard core for him.

Deciding that he might as well complete the set of Glug, Glug members, he hung around at the edge of an animated conversation between Sylvia Spraggon and the LaGardes.

"Stop hovering from foot to foot, man, and join us!" barked Sylvia.

"What do think of this? Californian gut rot if you ask me."

"Er, it's Italian actually. Primitivo."

"Even worse. Give me a good hard Stonker any day. You know Peter and Poppy, I suppose?" she said, winking at Tedesco.

Addressing the nouveau riche couple, Sylvia told them that Tedesco had just returned from Madeira.

"Bit of a coincidence, eh?" she added.

"I'm not sure what you mean, Sylvia," said a startled Poppy. "We've just got back from the Bahamas."

"But you know Madeira well, don't you, Mr Fairfax?" Sylvia said, with more than a hint of menace.

Poppy glanced at her watch.

"I think we need to go. I'm due at the gym."

The LaGardes made their excuses and left, leaving their unfinished glasses on a nearby table.

"Top marks for subtlety, Sylvia," said Tedesco.

"Thank you, kind sir," she replied. "Discretion isn't my middle name. It's Phaedra."

For reasons that, later, he couldn't explain apart from being an instinctive investigator's reaction, Tedesco crossed the room to examine the unfinished glasses before they were cleared away.

Peter and Poppy had both been drinking the Primitivo. Pete had barely sipped his, but Poppy's glass was interesting. There were clear signs of effervescence present in the remaining liquid.

Tedesco took the glass and sought out Canon Wilfred.

"This is going to sound bizarre, but is there somewhere that this glass can be kept safe, preferably under lock and key?"

"Leave it to me," Wilf replied.

Remembering that he hadn't spoken to either Martin Smedley or Stephen and Rachel Lowndes, he rejoined the throng.

Smedley had already retreated to his work in the cathedral archive, but the most boring couple in the wine club were still there, on their own.

Time to ask about Rachel's links with local landscape gardeners…

But before he could start to interrogate the architect, he became aware of a growing kerfuffle which was sweeping across the room like a tsunami.

It transpired that an ambulance had been called. Poppy LaGarde had fainted on her way to the car park in the Close, and that renowned medical expert Julie Stringer was soon busy telling anyone within hearing distance that she looked like she'd had a heart attack.

TWENTY-EIGHT

The Sanctuary of 17 St Budeaux Place

The wake had fully broken up by mid-afternoon and by the time Tedesco had finished helping Jos with the tedious task of clearing up the remaining wine bottles, he decided that it was hardly worth going back to work.

He called Sally, who was only too happy to close the office an hour early in return for agreeing to walk Barker round to Tedesco's house.

However, any hopes he was entertaining for a late-afternoon power nap were thwarted by an urgent succession of messages flashing up on his phone.

His sister wanted to know if it was true that there had been another murder – Julie Stringer had hinted to her that there had been.

He wisely resisted the temptation to respond to Nicky with sarcasm by saying that if Julie thought someone had been murdered, then there was no point in any further investigation.

He was cursing himself for accepting the invitation to join the Glug, Glug WhatsApp group – Poppy LaGarde was now in intensive care, if the rumours were to be believed, and the group chat was red-hot.

Stephen and Rachel wondered out loud if the members should be given police protection; Sylvia told them not to be snowflakes. The Claytons wanted to know if there were visiting hours in the ICU unit.

Once Sally had safely returned Barker home, Tedesco decided to switch off his phone and grab some sleep.

He must have been out for an hour or two when he was woken by a combination of a barking border terrier and some loud knocking on his door.

"Alright! Give me a minute!"

He bundled his sleepy body down the stairs and opened the door to his friend and business partner, the redoubtable Jos Elsted.

"Jos! You look terrible!"

The habitually well-coiffed wine merchant looked as if he had been dragged through a hedge backwards and he was clutching a plastic Morrison's carrier rather than his hand-stitched leather man bag.

"Just let me in, will you."

Once over the threshold, Jos bent down and apologised to Barker for startling him.

Barker did his level best to silently convey the message that assisting with human mental health issues formed a key element of his skill set.

"Have you heard?" Jos asked Tedesco. "Poppy LaGarde might be dead! The police will be on their way to arrest me!"

Tedesco led his friend into his private domain, the snug.

"And why would that be?" he asked, calmly.

"Because she drank some of my wine of course!"

"Yes, but that doesn't mean that it killed her, does it?

Look, I assume you are staying for supper so why don't I call The Rhyminster Raj and order some lamb dhansak?"

"Isn't that what they call our esteemed member of parliament – the Raj of Rhyminster?"

"Indeed, it is. But the best curry house in Devon was winning awards long before he arrived and it will be there long after he's gone. What shall we have to drink with it?"

Jos smiled. "I brought a couple of bottles of the white we were serving at the wake."

*

Poppy was pronounced dead later that evening.

The preliminary verdict was that she had been poisoned, and the police were awaiting the toxicology reports before deciding on the next steps.

Meanwhile, Tedesco and Elsted had made short work of the curry and the second bottle had been uncorked.

"Look, Jos, I get why you are so worried, but let's look at this logically. We were both busy talking to people at the wake – the cathedral refectory staff were serving the drinks as I recall – and so if someone happened to slip something into Poppy's drink, then it wasn't you or I."

"Yes, but won't people – and the police – put two and two together? Three poisonings of wine club members—"

Tedesco put his hand up as if he was halting traffic.

"But two of them were – possibly – poisoned with something in bottles of Madeira, which we don't supply, and as for Poppy, if it was a poisoning, then it was carried out in very different circumstances. If the first two were linked, this seems like it could be someone else."

"So what are you saying, John? The gluggers are bumping each other off?"

"Have you got a better theory? Look, why don't I see you safely home then we'll see what the morning brings."

Half an hour later, having literally dragged Jos back to his apartment in the Close, Tedesco decided that he would have a final glass of the serviceable Sauvignon that had been used at the wake.

He needed a suitable track to tie up his feelings at the end of this difficult day.

This case was getting harder to get to grips with, like trying to grab an eel in an oil slick. He felt like he was still starting out, feeling his way in the darkness.

He knew the perfect song now. It came from the master, the fount of all the great music that came in his wake.

Buddy Holly, 'Learning the Game'.

Barker seemed to agree with his choice as he curled up next to him.

"Shall I play it again, old friend?"

TWENTY-NINE

Glug, Glug Gate

DCI Tagg convened an urgent case review in the rear section of the first floor of the Bristol Road HQ, which had been converted into a somewhat Heath Robinson-style operation room.

Also present were DS Lovell and DC Sennen.

"So, to bring you up to speed, we now have three deaths. All of them were members of Glug, Glug and the initial report from the lab indicates that Poppy LaGarde was also poisoned, probably cyanide."

She paused to take a sip of water, then went on.

"The chief constable is taking an interest, and the media will be all over us. Apart from social media, I gather that Julie Stringer was present at the wake where Poppy was poisoned, and she is thick with Nicky Tedesco of BBC Searchlight, so it's odds on that their outside broadcast cameras will be turning up in front of the cathedral. Questions?"

"Yes, ma'am," said Jade Sennen. "Have the media made the connection with Glug, Glug?"

"Good point. Not yet, and we need to keep it that way, or else this will turn into Glug, Glug Gate. Matt?"

"One of the guests at the wake told me that the LaGardes made a somewhat panicked exit."

"Because Poppy was feeling faint," Tagg replied, a little brusquely.

"Yes, ma'am, but did you know that her husband had been having a decidedly animated conversation with one of the other gluggers?"

"Sylvia Spraggon would be my guess. Look, Tedesco took it upon himself to go to Madeira on the pretext of a mini-break, but while he was out there he was looking into allegations of aggressive selling of timeshares made by Miss Spraggon – never address her as 'Ms', whatever you do – and he discovered that Pete, who went by the name of Charles Fairfax back then, was one of the men involved."

"Do I assume that John was also investigating the Madeira wine angle?" asked Lovell.

"Of course he was, as he wanted to protect Jos Elsted and their business. And he came back with some theories about how cyanide could have been slipped into the wine. Jade, where are we with Mr Lowndes?"

"The prints we took from him match those found on the card attached to the gift box."

"Hmm. So we need to see him again. Bring him in for questioning later today. In the meantime, what do we all think?"

Matt Lovell kicked off. "Sylvia has got to be worth looking at, at least for Poppy. She had beef with Pete, and she was seen arguing with him just before the fainting episode. She might have intended the poison for him."

Tagg nodded encouragingly. "The old 'glasses switched by mistake' routine. Worth a punt."

She noticed that DC Sennen was bursting to speak.

"Jade?"

"But there is nothing to link her with Foster or Verity, is there? Stephen Lowndes clearly has questions to answer about Verity, but Foster? It could be almost any of them."

"Assuming that it was a glugger in the first place," said Lovell. "Foster wasn't exactly well liked."

Tagg thought for a moment.

"OK. We should avoid the lazy assumption that this is a serial operation, notwithstanding that all the deaths are of club members. It could be three individual killers, possibly acting together, or it may be more random. Can we rule out any of the gluggers at this stage?"

"Martin Smedley doesn't seem to have a motive," said Jade.

"Yeah but did you smell the inside of Foster's place?" said Lovell. "Smedley must have been there recently."

Tagg said, "I think we need to look at the poison. Who would have access to it?"

"The doctors," said Jade.

"Jim and Mary Clayton – they used to run a garden centre," said Matt.

"Good thinking," said Tagg. "Actually, John Tedesco said something that might be interesting. He was very keen to underline that Rachel Lowndes deals with large properties with landscaped gardens."

Jade's eyes lit up. "So she must deal with landscape gardeners! I assume they need to kill off noxious plants and so on?"

"Which means that she could have a means of acquiring poison as well!" said Lovell.

DCI Tagg paused before summarising what she had heard.

"OK, so we have several ideas about the cyanide, but we need to focus on two other aspects. First, the Madeira. Who got hold of it? How did Elsted's label get to appear on the bottles, when he evidently doesn't sell the stuff, and why is someone, or several someones, trying to pin the blame on him?

"And secondly, motive. I think we are looking at Spraggon and Lowndes as prime suspects at this stage, with the doctors, the Claytons and Rachel having question marks against them over supplying the cyanide – but Jackson could still be of interest, and poor old Jos needs to come up with an explanation for the prints on the labels."

"A tangled web, ma'am," said Lovell.

"Which we need to untangle. Let's get to it. We will start by searching the homes of all the gluggers."

THIRTY

A Speedy Discovery

DCI Tagg had been anticipating a long, drawn-out and possibly fruitless search of the various homes and haunts of the members of Glug, Glug.

So she was more than pleasantly surprised to find her pessimism to have been unjustified when Jade Sennen reported back on the search that been carried out at the Claytons' home in Woolford that very morning.

Jim had been absent from home, Mary explaining that he was taking a van load of garden waste to the tip, but that he would be back within the hour.

She was only too happy – eager, in fact – to assist in any way and gave the search team the full run of the house, including Jim's immaculately arranged garden shed.

Neatly packed away in the corner were two packets of Weed Murderer. A quick glance at the almost hysterical warnings on the front, complete with skull-and-crossbones insignia and a throat-slitting emoji, revealed that prussic acid was used in the manufacture, and that great care should be used when applying the treatment.

Jade recalled her initial visit to the lovely couple and how Weed Murderer had been mentioned in the context of weedkillers that might contain cyanide. The subject had come up, she remembered, because Jim had been asked for advice about irradicating giant hogweed from his garden by none other than Peter LaGarde. More than interesting.

Mary was visibly startled by the news that two packets of the stuff had been found on her property.

"I must have signed for them the other week. Jim is always ordering things, if not for him then for friends. He is an unofficial consultant to lots of amateur gardeners, you see. I wouldn't have looked closely at what they delivered. Weed Murderer – it's lethal in the wrong hands!"

"This must be a shock, Mary, but could any of these amateur gardeners include members of your wine society?"

*

Back in Rhyminster, Tedesco had texted Julia Tagg, copying in Canon Wilfred, to explain that the cathedral had safely secured the glass that had been found to have contained suspicious contents at Commander Foster's wake.

Tagg sent a uniformed officer straight round to Wilf's office to collect the item.

Lab testing would later reveal that the effervescence in the glass could have been down to the insertion of three granules of Weed Murderer, the brand of weedkiller that had been found in Jim Clayton's shed.

Meanwhile, back in Woolford, Jade didn't have long to wait before Jim Clayton returned from his visit to the tip.

After getting over his initial shock at finding a police car outside his house – "I thought something must have happened to Mary" – he calmed down and confirmed that he had ordered the toxic weedkiller, but it wasn't for Peter LaGarde. It was for a client of Rachel Lowndes.

"She needed it for some landscaping on a swish new barn conversion inland from Kingsbridge, she told me."

"So, when is she going to pick it up, or do you deliver it?" Jade asked.

"Funny you should ask – she knows it's arrived but hasn't made any arrangements."

"Why don't you and I go and have a closer look in the shed?"

"I'll put the kettle on," said the ever-patient Mary.

Jim led Jade back into his shed, where he shone a torch on the supposedly sealed packets. One of them had clearly been tampered with. It looked as if a small hole had been neatly inserted, or even drilled, enabling a tiny sample of the poison to be extracted.

"Who the hell did that?" said Jim.

"I'm going to have call in the hazmat suits to remove this safely. In the meantime, do not enter this shed. I assume you have a secure lock?"

*

As instructed by DCI Tagg at the case meeting, Lovell invited Stephen Lowndes to the station for questioning on his way home from school. Was he the 'Steve' on the card attached to the gift left for Verity?

Lowndes, at the wheel of Thunderbird One, drove into the station car park and tried to compose himself, telling himself that he had done nothing, had nothing to feel guilty about apart from falling in love with Verity and that he was a victim in this tragedy. He naïvely assumed that he was one of several wine club members being asked to help with enquiries prior to being eliminated from the investigation rather than being lined up as the prime suspect for the second death among the gluggers.

Facing Tagg and Lovell in the interview room, he was advised that the interview was to be under caution, and he was asked if wanted a lawyer present.

"Now wait a minute! I am here as a dutiful citizen, eager to help bring the killer to justice. Why the need for a lawyer?"

Lovell calmly repeated the statement of the interviewee's rights and offered to call the duty solicitor.

"No, thank you! Let's just get on with it. I need to get home – I've got a mountain of marking."

"Very well, Mr Lowndes. Now, for the tape, DCI Tagg is showing you a card."

"OK."

"And what does it say, sir?"

Lowndes' expression was hard to read. Was it genuine incomprehension, or was he looking a little bit shifty?

"You want me to read it out?"

"If you could."

Lowndes shrugged. "OK," he said, "'All my love, Steve.'"

"Are you known as Steve?" Tagg asked. "I have only ever heard you referred to as Stephen."

Lowndes considered his reply carefully. "Rachel calls me Steve sometimes."

"What about Verity Glynde?"

The primary school teacher looked like one of his pupils who had been caught red-handed and was making a pathetic attempt to cover up some minor misdemeanour.

"No. Why would she? Look, what is really behind this? Are you suggesting something untoward?"

"That's an interesting choice of words. A further question: do you recognise the writing on the card? Have another look if it helps."

"No need. It's my writing alright. I expect the card was attached to a present for Rachel."

"So it wasn't attached to a present for Verity?"

"No! Why on earth would I give a present to her? This is bonkers! Can I go now? I really have a ton of marking."

"OK, one more question. Were you having an affair with Verity?"

Lowndes stood up, the quiet mouse transformed into an angry tiger.

"You asked me if I needed a lawyer! I do now! This is slander. How dare you!"

Lovell managed to talk him down and regain his seat.

Tagg looked Stephen Lowndes firmly in the face. "You can go now, Stephen. But you should remain in the Rhyminster area while we continue our enquiries."

THIRTY-ONE

Rachel and Stephen: Not So Boring, Perhaps?

Tagg, Lovell and Sennen gathered in the makeshift incident room to compare notes.

Jade was eager to share the revelation about the Weed Murderer and the other two updated her on the interview with Lowndes.

"Matt, what did you think of him? He didn't try to hide the fact that he wrote 'All my love, Steve' on the card, did he?"

"I was impressed with that," Lovell replied, "but there was something about the way he answered your question about an affair with Verity. It seemed like genuine indignation, but what was your take?"

"Mmm. I couldn't tell if we had struck a nerve or if he really was outraged. If Lowndes hadn't attached the card to the gift to Verity, then who had and why were they making it look as if he had done it?"

Tagg noticed that Jade was eager to chip in, so she gestured for her to join the conversation.

"Someone was either trying to make it look like they – Steve and Verity – were having a fling or whatever or knew that they were and was trying to expose them."

"But would that extend to trying to kill Verity?" Lovell added.

"If it was the wronged wife who did it, then maybe."

Jade jumped in again. "Jim Lovell told me that Rachel Lowndes had ordered the weedkiller, but that she hadn't made arrangements to pick it up, remember."

Tagg got up and stood on one leg like a flamingo, a sure sign that she was having a deep think.

After thirty seconds, she reverted to her normal posture and gave her verdict.

"So, if we join up the dots, Rachel obtained the poison, added some crystals to a bottle of Madeira and was easily able to put her husband in the frame by attaching an old card that he had given her to the gift bag. And why would she want to do that?"

"Because her husband was at it with Verity!" exclaimed Jade, with a certain girlish enthusiasm.

"Or maybe she just convinced herself that he was. I thought that Lowndes seemed quite genuine when he denied it," said Lovell.

"OK, let's all sleep on this. It seems more than a bit too plausible for my liking. We will need to talk to Rachel Lowndes, that much is clear. But a couple of things bother me. Why didn't she collect the poison from Jim? Why go through the rigmarole of siphoning it off, presumably after breaking into the shed? Would she really do that? And wasn't her attempt to frame her husband, if that was what it was, a bit obvious, a bit clumsy?"

With that, DCI Tagg strode to the door, then turned around and told the others to head home. Tomorrow was going to be a busy day. And she would love to be a fly on the wall at the Lowndes household this evening.

She wasn't going straight home though. She drove through the Close and turned into St Budeaux Place. Time to pick the brains of the finest detectives she knew: Barker and Tedesco.

Barker, his ears attuned to any movement in the mews, was at the door to greet his friend Julia Tagg as soon as she knocked on Tedesco's door.

"Hello, Barker! I've come to pick your brains, and John's as well. Is he in?"

The polite border terrier led her into the den, where Tedesco was engaged in yet another reclassification of his prized vinyl album collection. She immediately noticed that he had a glass of red wine resting on the side table.

"Jools! I didn't hear you!"

"But your fierce guard dog did. Am I disturbing you?"

"No, no. Just trying to resolve the age-old problem. Do I file the solo albums of the members of the Fab Four under The Beatles, or under their own initials."

"Wow. I can see that you have your work cut out there. Could you spare me a few minutes?"

Tedesco indicated the sofa. "Of course. I don't suppose I can tempt you to a glass of red. Jos has asked me to test it – Slovenian."

"I'm not on duty, but I am driving. And I've had way too much coffee today, so perhaps we can just crack on? It's about the wine club deaths, of course."

"I thought as much. I think I had better top up my glass if murder is on the agenda."

He popped into the kitchen, brandishing the remains of the bottle.

"Interesting grape variety, bit short though. Sorry, let's stick to the wine club."

Tagg updated him as far as she felt able to, and Tedesco listened intently before commenting.

"As you have intimated, the wronged wife theory seems a bit too convenient, I think. And what about Foster and Poppy LaGarde? Are we saying that if Rachel was the source of the poison, she could also be in the frame for those two as well?"

"That's pretty much what I was wondering. But we don't actually know that Rachel was the person who ordered the weedkiller."

"You only have Jim Clayton's word on that. And I suppose any invoice would be made out to him."

"Good point. We can dig deeper. I'm taking Jade Sennen with me to see Rachel tomorrow."

"I assume you will be asking her about any affair?"

"Once we've confronted her about the poison, yes. John, have you picked up anything new?"

"Not news, exactly, but my excitable neighbour Sylvia invited me round for a glass of Stonker – please don't ask – and she was seeking reassurance that she wasn't going to be charged for the murder of Poppy. By the way, do you know if it was the wine that killed her? The white wine we served at Foster's wake?"

"Full toxicology report due any moment, but that is our working assumption."

Tedesco took another sip of his wine. "Hmm, not sure I can mark this at more than a five. Anyway, Sylvia was ripped off by timeshare touts in Madeira, as you know."

"And one of them might have been Pete LaGarde."

"So why did Poppy get murdered?"

"What do you and Jos think? I presume you have discussed it?"

"Of course. And Jos is more than aware that he looks suspicious having supplied the wine. We wonder if the wine glasses were swapped, either deliberately or by accident."

"So Pete was the intended victim. This doesn't look great for Sylvia."

"But how would she have got hold of the poison, let alone come up with the idea?"

Tagg got up to go. "Lots to think about. Will you keep me in the picture?"

"I've just had my latest invitation to the monthly Glug, Glug meeting. We are testing some wines that might be good for Christmas. Jos will be introducing them."

"A good opportunity to assess the mood of the members."

"Jools, I am treating it as a deadline. The meeting is in three weeks' time."

"So, what, you are going to go all Hercule Poirot, are you? The suspects all gathered in one place; you go round the room assessing their culpability before revealing the murderer!"

"Yes, that is absolutely my plan. I have been rereading the great Agatha and it struck me that this could work in this unique set of circumstances."

Tagg smiled indulgently.

"And how strong is that wine you are drinking?"

THIRTY-TWO

The Dots Won't Join Up

Had DCI Tagg been a fly on any one of the walls of the Lowndes' nondescript house, she would have overheard a difficult exchange.

Despite his detention at the police station, Stephen was still home before Rachel, who almost drove Thunderbird Two into the garage door before launching a verbal assault against her hapless husband.

"Oh, is that something nice I can smell in the oven? You forgot to turn it on, didn't you? Why I married such a spineless loser I will never know. Can you even use a mobile? You'd better order us a takeaway. Bloody hell, Stephen! All I need after my day!"

Stephen stood up and told Rachel to sit down and be quiet.

"I have been at the police station – thanks for asking about my day. And I must not leave the Rhyminster area until they have completed their wretched enquiries."

"Why the hell not? What have you told them? I hope you asked for a solicitor."

She paused for effect.

"Of course you didn't. You total wimp. What the hell have you told them, Stephen?"

"The truth."

"Oh, God. Spit it out, the suspense is killing me."

"Perhaps we can start by you telling me the truth. How did a card I wrote for you end up being attached to a gift to Verity. It was discovered at her flat after she was murdered."

"Was she murdered? I have no idea about a card. You must have written it for her. You were shagging her, weren't you, or have I got that wrong as well?"

"What Verity and I had was beautiful. How dare you make it sound sordid."

"Whatever. Once you've had supper, I think you'd better move out for a while. The Travelodge is quite near your school."

"No way. I'm the good guy here. You tried to make it look like I killed her, but the police will see through it. What I will do is move into the spare room. Final answer. And you'd better steel yourself for a visit: they believed me."

"What, when you denied that you and that awful hippy were an item? I assume that you lied about it."

"Think what you want. And I'm not hungry. Order your own sodding takeaway."

*

Tagg couldn't sleep, and so she went for a run. She was in the station before Sennen and Lovell and was straining to get down to work. She had pondered on what she had heard the previous evening and now she had a game plan.

"Jade, I want you to come with me. We will surprise Rachel Lowndes at her office. I'll brief you on the way.

Matt, could you call on the Claytons? Ask Jim if he has any paperwork relating to the order for the weedkiller. His wife told us that Jim was an unofficial consultant to various local gardeners. Ask him for a list of them and whether anyone has access to the shed, or if he hides a key somewhere. Oh, and if our friend Greville Jackson happens to be one of these amateur horticulturists, then it might be worth paying him a call. We can't let him think that he's been forgotten."

Lovell grinned. "He'd be difficult to forget! I'd better see him before lunch – I expect he starts to hit the vino early."

DCI Tagg and DC Sennen endured a difficult morning while they waited at Rachel's architects' practice. Her PA, who had clearly been primed, tried to stall them by saying that Rachel was at a site meeting. Sennen had already spotted Thunderbird Two in the car park, so the detectives said they would wait.

After an hour, Rachel appeared from a meeting room with two smartly dressed clients, but she couldn't avoid going through reception as she showed them out.

"Good meeting, was it, Mrs Lowndes?" said Tagg. "Let us introduce ourselves."

Meanwhile, DS Lovell was sitting in the conservatory of the Clayton residence, tucking into Mary's delicious Dundee cake.

Jim had been sent off to find the paperwork for the weedkiller, so Lovell took the opportunity to ask Mary about access to the shed.

"We do keep a set of spare keys in the porch, which is never locked. Just in case we lock ourselves out, you see, and we sometimes let old friends from Lancashire stay here when we are on holiday. Kind of a house-sitting arrangement, if you know what I mean."

"Is that safe?"

Mary laughed. "They are kept in one of Jim's old wellies, under a pair of worn-out socks. They are well hidden!"

"Does the set include a key to the shed?"

"Oh yes. Jim uses the spare one quite often. Oh, and if the house is going to be empty, Mark and Sue have a full set. They live in the village, you know."

Jim reappeared clutching some invoices. "Here it is – the order for the Weed Murderer."

"Could I take a photo of that, please?"

"Be my guest. You can take the original if you like, I've got a copy on file."

"Great. Now, I expect you both know where these questions are leading to?"

"Aye. How did some bugger break into my shed and drill a hole in the weedkiller?"

"Jim! I must excuse my husband's language."

Lovell smiled. "I've heard far worse, believe me. Anyway," he continued, "Mrs Clayton told us that you act as a kind of unofficial consultant to various local gardeners."

Clayton nodded.

"Do you have a list of these people?"

"Not written down, like. But I can run through them. There's Greville Jackson at the Grange, of course. He hasn't got a clue about that lawn of his. Then there is Mr LaGarde, poor chap. Even more clueless than Greville. He had a problem with giant hogweed the other year. Bloody awful stuff, like something out of *The Day of the Triffids*. The sap stinks to high heaven and burns you if you touch it."

Mary butted in like a prompter in a stage play.

"And there's Rachel as well, isn't there, love."

"Er, of course. She and her grand projects!"

"And was one these projects a barn conversion? Near Kingsbridge?"

Jim looked to his prompt again before replying.

"Aye, I think she ordered the weedkiller for her clients. Japanese knotweed, I seem to remember."

"We will ask her. Thank so much for your time. And for the cake. Mary, your baking is one of the few aspects of this investigation that I relish."

As he exited the bungalow, Lovell resisted the temptation to look back. He expected that there would be some awkward conversations.

At least one of these outwardly harmless retirees was telling porkies.

Over at the architects' practice, Rachel Lowndes had opted to turn on the professional charm, apologising profusely for the wait and offering tea and coffee and the use of the boardroom.

Neither of the police officers were taken in by this, and both noticed how quickly Rachel started to blame her poor PA for failing to find her as soon as they had arrived.

Tagg opened the bowling by explaining that they were here to ask Rachel if she would help them with their enquiries into the recent death of Verity Glynde.

This didn't appear to faze her. "Can we do this here?"

"Oh yes, this is an informal discussion," Tagg said.

"You see, it appears that a substance found in certain types of weedkiller may have been the cause of death," she added.

"And how can I possibly assist you?"

Sennen explained that as Rachel was a landscape expert,

she wondered whether she had to use, or recommend to clients, special treatments for invasive species.

Rachel thought carefully before replying.

"Very occasionally, but I really cannot recall the last time. As I am sure you know, invasive species like knotweed and so on require expert treatment and certification."

"Thank you, Mrs Lowndes. Now, would you ever consult a local horticulturist, Jim Clayton perhaps, on the type of treatment to apply?"

"Heavens no! We have our own professional consultants. I like Jim, he's a real character, but all he did is run a garden centre up north. And you need to be regulated to supply this type of stuff. I doubt very much if he is."

"Very helpful," said Tagg. "Now, we don't want to hold you up any longer, but we do have a couple of final questions."

Rachel Lowndes sat up and straightened her skirt.

Jade asked the first question. "Are you currently advising on a barn conversion near Kingsbridge?"

"No."

Tagg asked the final question. "Has your husband ever cheated on you?"

"Yes."

THIRTY-THREE

A Catch-up with Greville Jackson

As he braced himself for the hazardous private drive and prayed for his car's suspension, Lovell soon realised that the only means of vehicular access to Woolford Grange was now even more potholed, rutted and hazardous than the last time he had visited.

He made his uncertain way towards the gravel circle which signalled the end of the ordeal and thought he heard the sounds of gunshot mingled with shouting.

Parking a safe distance from Jackson's battered Range Rover, he exited the car just as the barnacled old aristocrat emerged from the undergrowth, rifle in hand, followed by his cowed-looking black Labrador.

"Smollett! When I issue the command 'Attack!', I mean bite the bounder in the bollocks, not lick him!"

Noticing Lovell's arrival, he swivelled and pointed the gun at the intruder.

"Smollett, attack!"

The dog slunk up to Lovell, who stroked him.

"Get off my land, you pustular excrescence! Now!"

Lovell, who was actually quite scared, produced his warrant card.

"What's that you are waving at me? Your student railcard?"

Lovell girded his loins and approached Greville Jackson. "It is my warrant card. And please put that firearm away or else you will be charged with threatening an officer of the law. And we have met before."

"What! Maybe. Love, did you say were called?"

Ignoring this, Lovell told Jackson that he would appreciate his help in answering some questions relating to the death of Verity Glynde.

On the drive over to Woolford, Lovell had remembered the various accounts from Glug, Glug members of Jackson's appalling rudeness to Verity, culminating in his outburst at Foster's final meeting when she had the temerity to raise the subject of the club taking a 'dry' January break.

So Jackson's reaction to his suggestion came as no surprise to him.

"You would appreciate my help, would you? Well, I would appreciate some help from your lot. Why aren't you looking into the poachers, eh? And as for 'Ms' Glynde, if she wasn't knocked unconscious by one of her wind chimes or overcome with the aroma of joss sticks, I think you should be looking at sex!"

"You will need to explain that comment, Mr Jackson."

"Gordon Bennett! I am referring to motive, you idiot. It's always either sex or money, and that dreamcatcher in human form was always wittering on about the dangers of materialism. So look at sex!"

"Are you suggesting that Verity had a lover, Mr Jackson? Was it you?"

Lovell had inserted that suggestion as much for his own amusement as anything else and was rewarded by an inarticulate rant of epic proportions, the nub of which was that Jackson hadn't exactly found the deceased to be in any way alluring and that he had formed the working assumption that she was a lesbian.

Once the rant had subsided, Lovell calmly asked Jackson if he could sit down inside with him as he was interviewing all the members and he really didn't want to have to ask him to come to the station.

"Bloody hell! Oh well, let's get it over with. At least you can tick me off your list, I suppose."

Jackson led his guest into the cluttered kitchen via the antler-infested entrance hall and offered Lovell a choice of red or white.

"I am on duty, sir. But some water would be good."

Jackson tutted. "Our old village bobby, PC Cottingham, he was always pissed as a newt. And do you know what the crime rate was in those days? Zero."

After turfing the long-suffering Smollett out into the garden – "He farts a lot" – Jackson turned to Lovell.

"Well? I haven't got all day. What do you want to know?"

"Thank you, Mr Jackson. You have a large acreage here. Have you ever had a problem with invasive species?"

"Apart from poachers, or wankers in anoraks who insist on exercising their so-called 'right to roam'?"

Lovell interrupted what he expected was going to be a long list of groups who met with Jackson's disapproval.

"I was thinking more of bindweed, for example. Knotweed even?"

"Wouldn't know. Just let things grow wild."

"So you haven't ordered any weedkiller? I gather that Jim Clayton advises you about gardening matters."

"He tells me when to put a ton of shit on the roses and so on."

"So you haven't ordered any supplies of weedkiller from him?"

Jackson looked at Lovell with disdain.

"No, why the hell would I? Look, do you have any relevant questions?"

The landline rang.

"Bally thing! Hang on while I deal with this."

Jackson strode up to the old-fashioned receiver and barked into it, "Adolf Hitler's phone! Ha! They rang off. Always works. Probably criminals. I'd get rid of the line but the mobile coverage out here is lavatorial."

He glared at Lovell.

"Next question!"

"Thank you, sir. In fact, your previous answer was very useful. I'd like to ask about your cellar and in particular about the bottles of Madeira that my colleague found there. Who supplies the wine? Jos Elsted?"

Jackson gave a petulant shrug. "And your point is?"

Lovell thought carefully before continuing.

"There is a Madeira aspect to the investigation, but please could you keep this to yourself."

Jackson barged in. "I know there is. Sylvia told me that the retired lawyer, Jim Tredegar, is investigating."

"He is called John Tedesco, sir, but do carry on."

"Anyway, this lawyer fellow went out to Madeira and found out that LaGarde – frightful little man – was behind the timeshare scam that poor old Sylvia was hoodwinked by. So he could be behind the murders."

"An interesting theory, sir. But you haven't answered my question. Where do you get your Madeira from?"

"Elsted doesn't stock it. So I get it delivered direct from

the island. My old friend Reggie Challenor lives out there and he has excellent contacts."

"I see. But why do you keep such a large stock – it can't be for your sole use?"

"Of course not! Do you think I'm some sort of dipsomaniac? I have an annual Christmas drinks party, and I make sure all the guests leave with a bottle of Madeira. It's a tradition."

"And would your guests include the members of Glug, Glug, Mr Jackson?"

"Some of them, yes. What do you want, a list?"

"That would be most helpful."

Jackson went into his study, sat at his escritoire and tried to remember which gluggers had attended the last drinks party. It was easier to remember who he hadn't invited – Martin Smedley, the awful LaGardes, the Glynde woman and Foster.

Meanwhile, Lovell strolled out into the garden and remade his acquaintance with Smollett. He was a very friendly dog and deserved a more sympathetic owner than Jackson.

DS Lovell ended his short break from duty and returned to the house just as Greville was ready to hand over his list.

Once he had fully deciphered the hieroglyphics, Lovell noted that none of the victims had been included on the guest list. This was interesting. What was even more notable were the names of the others who had been excluded from the festive fun.

Peter LaGarde and Martin Smedley. Could they be the next in line for the serial killer, if it was a series of connected murders that they were looking at?

THIRTY-FOUR

In the Refectory

Tedesco told Sally that he would be popping over to the cathedral, and that she would be left in charge of Barker.

"You haven't been over there for a while," said the long-serving PA. "I hope there haven't been any more murders or other incidents?"

The mention of 'incidents' was Sally's inept reference to her boss and his last investigation in the environs of the cathedral and its magnificent close, when he had found himself looking into a steamy affair, at least by Rhyminster standards, between two of the more prominent residents.

"So sorry to let you down, Sally. I'm just going to have coffee and a catch-up with Canon Wilfred, if that's alright with you."

"Touchy today," Sally muttered under her breath as Tedesco made his way down the rickety stairs, waving at Jos Elsted as they passed.

Canon Wilfred Drake, the cathedral precentor – in charge of the worship and music side of things – was, along with Jos, Tedesco's best pal in Rhyminster and the closest thing he had to a spiritual adviser, not that he would admit to needing one.

It had been Canon Wilf who had suggested the meeting in the cathedral's splendid refectory, which, as well as offering views of the tower through its glass roof, supplied its own brand of breakfast tea, Minster Blend, a pot of which was just being delivered as Tedesco sat down at the table with his friend.

"Sorry! I have kept you waiting!" Tedesco said.

"Just got here. I hope you don't mind – I ordered the usual."

"I'd expect nothing more. Shall I pour?"

After the routine pleasantries had been duly dealt with, Canon Wilf leaned in.

"John, I would value your opinion on something. Do you know Martin Smedley?"

"The archivist? Yes, I know him a little bit. He is a fellow member of a wine interest group that Jos introduced me to."

"Yes, I know. And I am aware of the shocking coincidence that links membership of Glug, Glug with the recent deaths. Martin came to see me about his deep anxiety about this. I'm not breaking the seal of the confessional, as he agreed to my discussing this with you. In fact, he asked me to do so, as he guessed that you would be looking into it."

"I'm flattered, and I'm not surprised to hear that poor Martin is anxious. All of the members are worried. Jos isn't sleeping, and even Sylvia is admitting to feeling vulnerable. So, what is Martin saying?"

"As you know him, you will be aware of the body odour problem."

Tedesco nodded.

"Martin says that it is a medical issue. All sorts of well-meaning people, including your PA, have suggested various deodorants and herbal remedies, but none of them have worked and Martin is, frankly, somewhat fed up with people trying to help. It just makes him even more self-conscious."

"It must be awful. I will have a quiet word with Sally. I expect she offered him some variation of a medieval nettle-based potion or a set of crystals."

"Ever the cynical lawyer, Mr Tedesco. Anyway, Martin has been interviewed by the police."

"As have all the other members of Glug, Glug, so he shouldn't feel in any way singled out."

"Good to know. Anyway, the subject of his, er, rather unique bouquet came up. Not to put too fine a point on it, when the police entered Commander Foster's house, the whole place reeked of it."

"Eau de Smedley. I see. So he is worried that this might suggest that he must have been at Foster's place around the time he died?"

"Indeed. I couldn't very well ask Martin, but I assume that the police will look into how long the stench lasts."

"It seems to be ever present in the cathedral archives. But even if Martin had been at the property at the crucial time, this doesn't prove anything. It is purely circumstantial."

"That's what I told him. But he is still terrified about being interviewed again."

"OK, let's consider what they might want to know. Did Foster and Martin hit it off? Might Martin have given the Commander a lift to the meeting on the night in question?"

"They have already asked him about the Glug, Glug meeting. Martin and Foster did get on quite well and Martin did pick him up and take him to the tastings, but Martin is adamant that Dr Elphick gave Foster a lift to Woolford on that particular evening."

"Which Dr Elphick?"

"Dr Susan."

"Interesting. Did Martin know why Foster accepted a lift from her?"

"He didn't say. To be fair, I didn't think to ask him."

Tedesco, sensing that there was more to come, said, "Go on."

"He did tell me something which might have a bearing on things. A few days before the meeting, Dr Sue rang him, ostensibly to check that he was going to the meeting, but then she asked him to keep an eye on Commander Foster as she had noted that he had appeared to be feeling isolated and in need of company."

"But why would that be of interest? Dr Sue was acting like an old-fashioned GP, caring for her patients in the round. I don't actually know if Foster and Smedley were on her patient list, but she knows them from Glug, Glug and was probably just trying to get two lonely men to meet up for some company. Maybe over a glass of wine, as they had wine tasting in common."

"Perhaps it's my chance to be cynical, John. It also gave Martin the opportunity to visit Foster and, to be frank, leave his mark."

"And thus put the police off the scent if someone else had killed the Commander."

The two friends were momentarily silenced as they thought this through, Tedesco breaking the spell by offering to pour a second cup.

Then he spoke.

"Wilf, I am working in the background with Julia Tagg on this. She asked me to."

Canon Wilfred smiled. "I knew she would. Nothing moves in this city without you, and Barker of course, knowing about it."

"Border terriers are very intuitive, actually," said Tedesco.

"What I was wondering," he went on, "is whether I should share what we have discussed with Jools. I think this might help Martin."

"In that case, share away," said the precentor, who then excused himself as he was running late for a meeting with the Master of Musick.

Tedesco resolved to leave the office early that afternoon. WFH – working from home – was a thing nowadays, and so he decided that he could do with minimal distraction to enable him to write up the latest developments in his blue counsel's notebook. These books, with perforated edges to each page, were used in solicitors' offices and barristers' chambers.

Ever since founding the agency, he had written up his notes for each case in a box-fresh counsel's notebook, writing the title of the investigation in block capitals on the front cover and then completing his notes in his beautiful copperplate handwriting.

Once he had completed that vital but painstaking task, he would contact DCI Tagg and see if she was free for a meeting on neutral ground.

When Lynne Davey worked with him, they found it useful to meet off site at the Kingfisher pub on the River Rhyme. He hadn't been for a while…

THIRTY-FIVE

Déjà Vu at the Kingfisher

"Where are you off to at this hour?" said Barker's expression. "I am a dog and I need a regular routine."

Sensing his best friend's puzzlement, Tedesco explained that he was off to meet Julia Tagg.

"You like Jools, don't you, Barker? I've left your supper, and I promise not to stay out late. And I will tune the radio to Classic FM."

This was Barker's preferred listening of choice.

The border terrier stretched and made for his basket.

As it was a dry, clear evening, Tedesco walked to the Kingfisher, Rhyminster's attempt at a gastropub, his route taking him back through the Close and then along the path through the water meadows.

He would probably take a taxi home.

The pub, perfectly located on a bend of the River Rhyme, looked welcoming as he ducked under the ancient beams and made his way to the bar. There was no sign of DCI Tagg, so he ordered himself a large glass of Pinot noir. Noticing that there was a copy of the *Rhyminster Journal* on the counter, he took it and headed for a discreet booth where he and Jools could enjoy a view of the evening light on the river.

Opening the paper, he turned immediately to the 'It Makes Me Mad!' column, Julie Stringer's increasingly bizarre take on the vagaries of twenty-first-century Rhyminster.

This week, she was recounting a story she had heard in one of the local eateries. A customer had ordered a dessert called 'Heart Attack on a Plate', and as no coronary was forthcoming, the matter had been reported to Trading Standards.

This reminded Tedesco of a short-lived restaurant near the station, called 'Lecters'. The naïve owners had thought that they had come up with the perfect name for their vegan eatery, as it would appeal to lovers of the delectable, hence 'Lecters'.

Apparently, the name Hannibal Lecter meant absolutely nothing to them and after a few weeks of dealing with people calling in asking if they sold fava beans, or turning up wearing face muzzles, they decided to shut up shop and try their luck elsewhere. Hopefully somewhere with a new name above the door.

"Sorry to keep you, John. Hardly had time to get home and change. This job!"

"I've only just got here myself," said Tedesco. "I've been catching up with Julie Stringer and her deranged ravings."

Jools laughed. "She's alright – in small doses perhaps. Anyway, you hinted that you may have some new insights into you know what."

Tedesco smiled. "I was hoping that we could share our findings. What can I get you?"

Jools was driving, and it was a school night, so she

opted for a zero per-cent ale brewed by Rhyme Ales, called 'Lightweight'.

Drink in hand, she came to the point.

"The lab tests were pretty clear. All three of them – Foster, Verity and Poppy – were the victims of poisoning."

"Sparkling cyanide – no surprise there."

"So, where did the murderer, or murderers, get hold of the stuff?"

Tedesco listened intently as DCI Tagg summarised the investigations into the source of the poison, how a somewhat dodgy garden product called Weed Murderer had assumed significance and how a stash of the stuff had been discovered, tampered with, in Jim Clayton's shed.

"How interesting. But who would have got hold of it, and what was their motive?" said Tedesco, speaking his thoughts out loud.

Jools gave a precis of where they were. "They could all have done it or been involved. Jackson held a Christmas drinks party last year, where he invited all the members of Glug, Glug with the exception of the victims and Peter LaGrande and Martin Smedley."

"So those two could be next?"

"We can't discount it. And Jackson gave each of his guests a parting festive gift."

"Let me guess. A bottle of Madeira?"

"Correct. So, if all of the wine club members had a bottle…"

"Any one of them could have used it in the murders. Or to send us off on a wild goose chase."

"Just to make things more complicated, Stephen Lowndes apparently addressed a card to Verity which was attached to the bottle found outside her apartment. It said, 'All my love, Steve.'"

"Do you think they were…"

"He denies it, but I wasn't convinced. But if he and Verity were an item, why on earth would he poison her?"

"Have you spoken to Rachel?"

Jools raised an eyebrow. "Oh yes. And Jim Clayton said that he had advised her about horticultural matters in connection with her practice."

"So she could have asked him about weedkillers?"

She nodded. "But she vehemently denies it. Then there's Sylvia, of course. She has motive, at least as far as Pete LaGarde is concerned."

"And she could have bodged the attempt to kill him, so Poppy swallowed the poison instead."

"I think I need another drink. Jools?"

"A pint of this stuff is more than enough. It's OK, but it seems to be missing something."

"Alcohol, perhaps?"

When Tedesco returned from the bar, he immediately noted a new caution in Jools's demeanour.

"I don't think they've seen us, but the two doctors have just been shown to a table. Why don't we discuss pleasantries and then drink up? I can drive you home and you can tell me what you have got on the way."

After Jools had told Tedesco about her hilarious weekend in Bristol with Lynne Davey – his former partner in the detective agency – and her now-husband Duncan Chivers, they crept out of the pub undetected.

Once in the car, Tedesco outlined what Wilf had told him about Smedley.

Tagg took this in, then she asked, "Do you think Smedley was getting his defence in first? I mean, if he had done it, his unique calling card would have implicated him, so he may have thought it a smart move to pretend to be worried that by visiting Foster out of the kindness of his heart, he had accidently made himself look guilty."

"Hmm," said Tedesco, as the car turned into the Close. "I'm not sure. I trust Wilf's antennae and he thought that Smedley was genuinely worried. Why did Dr Sue give Foster a lift on the fateful night? That's what I want to know."

"She was cagey about it when we interviewed her."

John let himself back in to his cosy bolthole and, trying not to wake Barker, went straight to his desk and updated his case notes.

As he inscribed his findings, he felt a surge of optimism that he might still be able to unearth the perpetrator at the next Glug, Glug meeting. He was increasingly confident that it was a single person.

Then, having closed the counsel's notebook for the night and headed up the stairs, he suddenly remembered something that he should have included.

The appearance of the Drs Elphick in the bar of the Kingfisher – how certain could he really be that they hadn't seen him?

THIRTY-SIX

The Grieving Widower

DCI Tagg had deliberately left the questioning of Peter LaGarde till later in the investigation to give him at least a short time to come to terms with the sudden and tragic death of his wife.

She delegated the task to Matt Lovell and suggested that he took Jade with him. The young DC had grown in confidence during the investigation and seemed to be thriving under pressure.

Trying to pin LaGarde down was proving quite difficult. The original smooth operator, he never seemed to be in one place for long.

Lovell eventually tracked him down and arranged to see him at his huge purpose-built mansion overlooking the River Dart.

In complete contrast to the drive leading to Greville Jackson's house, this one was perfectly gravelled, with dwarf lights illuminating the way.

Lovell tried and failed to suppress a smile.

"Something amusing you?" asked Jade.

"I was just imagining what Greville Jackson would

make of this place. He'd probably describe it as vulgar, like a footballer's house."

"Or like one of the judges' houses on *The X Factor*. Or maybe not. He isn't exactly up on popular culture. That said, I wouldn't mind living here. Do you think they've got an indoor pool?"

"Probably. And a gym, home cinema, spa. Makes you sick."

"But he's just lost his wife, don't forget."

Having thought that they had come to the end of the enormous drive, they found themselves approaching some impressive 'fuck off' security gates, through which they could see that the drive took a further turn before eventually leading to the gleaming, modern, stately home.

Lovell stopped at the gate, pressed the intercom and the huge gates parted like the Red Sea, closing behind them with an almighty clang as soon as the car had squeezed through.

LaGarde's housekeeper was waiting in pole position on the ostentatious outside steps, and she greeted the pair of detectives with a distinct lack of the milk of human kindness.

Lovell and Sennen were brusquely ushered into a waiting room, which resembled the reception area of a faceless corporate hotel.

Lovell noted that the reading matter for the LaGardes' guests was limited to *Men's Health* magazine and *Hello!*.

After what seemed like several hours' wait, but which in reality was probably only twenty minutes, they were collected and admitted into a large study, which boasted a feature fireplace and a huge window overlooking the vast garden. Sennen couldn't resist peering at the view just as a deer ran off into the woods.

LaGarde was sitting behind a vast faux-antique desk. He didn't stand up but gestured to the detectives to take the two chairs facing opposite him.

Lovell recognised the power dynamic and the need to confront it.

As the CID man began by thanking his host for agreeing to meet at this difficult time, LaGarde interrupted him.

"What took you so long? My wife was murdered. I assume you have come to tell me that you've made an arrest."

Sennen answered, speaking softly.

"We wanted to leave you to grieve, sir."

This disarmed LaGarde to an extent. "Oh, well, I suppose you were trying to be kind. But that doesn't answer my question. Have you arrested anyone?"

"Our enquiries are ongoing, Mr LaGarde," Lovell replied, adding that the matter was being treated as a top priority.

LaGarde stood up suddenly, another power play.

"Are you stupid? I have worked out who did it, so why haven't you?"

Noting that LaGarde had lost his customary sparkle, Lovell let him go on.

"So when are you going to arrest him? Elsted!"

Lovell had wondered where this had been heading. His money had been on Jackson as LaGarde's suspect, as there was no love lost between the two men, representing as they did the polar opposite forces of old and new money.

As the detectives maintained their tactical silence, LaGarde set out his reasoning.

"Elsted supplied the wine! It poisoned my wife! And isn't it a bit of a coincidence that Foster and Verity were both members of Glug, Glug? Elsted is a monster! A serial killer!

Look. The chief constable is a mate of mine. I think I'll give him a bell, see if he can stick a rocket up your arses."

Lovell took a deep breath. After all, he'd heard that old chestnut several times before.

"Have you quite finished, sir? I understand that you are still coming to terms with the tragedy, but bandying serious allegations around isn't helpful."

Jade, sensing that she was being nudged to join in, explained that LaGarde was correct in that three stalwarts of the wine group had died in suspicious circumstances, so it was – "I hope you agree" – surely right that they should interview all of the members.

"Perhaps we could start again. Do you have any reason to think anyone would want to kill Mrs LaGarde?"

The pugnacious entrepreneur visibly shrank back into his opulent chair.

"No," he whispered. "She was loved by everyone. She had no enemies."

"Mr LaGarde, did your wife have any medical conditions which could have made her more susceptible to the effects of having her drink spiked?"

"No! She was fighting fit. She has an annual check-up with Mark Elphick. Ask him if you don't believe me."

Lovell made a mental note to remember this and then he readied himself before asking the trickiest question.

"And you, sir? I have to ask this. Did you have any reason to doubt your wife? Had you been encountering any difficulties?"

LaGarde stood up again, furious.

"What are you suggesting? That Poppy was being unfaithful!"

"Please sit down, sir. I didn't mention infidelity."

LaGarde slowly sank back into his chair again, like a boxer who was struggling to stay on his feet.

"I was the one who cheated, not my Poppy. But she always took me back. Says a lot about someone, doesn't it. Look, can we wrap this up? I've got a funeral to arrange."

Sennen gave him her best empathetic smile.

"Of course, sir. And will the funeral be held locally?"

"No, it fucking well won't. It's in London, back to her roots. Plumed horses, open carriage, the works. And we won't be ordering the wine from Elsted."

Once they had cleared the security gates on the return journey, the detectives began to relax and review what they had just heard.

"What was your key learning point from Mr LaGarde, DC Sennen?"

"Infidelity, sir. As you said to him, you didn't mention it. So why did he?"

*

Meanwhile, at Minster Precincts, Jos Elsted was blissfully unaware of the contents of Peter LaGarde's accusations as he made his way down the rickety stairs to call in on his partner in 'Crime and Wine', John Tedesco.

"Jos! The kettle has just boiled and Sally is taking Barker for a walk around the Close, so we've got the place to ourselves. Is this just a social call?"

The kindly wine merchant smiled as if all was well with the world and God was in his heaven. But it clearly wasn't.

"It is about the murders. I can barely concentrate on anything else at the moment."

"*Anch'io*," said Tedesco.

"Eh?" said Jos.

"Sorry. It means 'me as well'. I slipped into Italian. It's a nervous thing."

"A pretentious thing," said Jos, chuckling.

"So, what's bothering you, old friend?"

"Probably nothing. It's about Dr Sue. She came into the shop to discuss the wines for our next tasting. It wasn't that long after the latest death, and when I mentioned to her what a shock it was that Poppy had died, she, I don't know, just seemed to sort of shrug, and, well, I'm not sure how to explain it, she looked winded. As I said, it probably meant nothing. I may have just imagined it…"

THIRTY-SEVEN

Once More Into the Incident Room

DCI Tagg, DS Lovell and DC Sennen gathered in front of a whiteboard which featured all the names of the gluggers inscribed in marker pen.

All of them had been interviewed either formally or informally since Poppy's death, with the exception of the Drs Elphick.

"Are they really worth seeing now?" asked Jade.

Lovell spoke up in support of his junior colleague. "This isn't like collecting those World Cup football stickers, is it? We don't need to collect the full set, do we? We have got so much on the others, and now we know that the poison came from Jim Clayton and not from the surgery."

Tagg put up her hand, as if she was on traffic duty.

"Hang on a minute. The poison may have been found in Clayton's shed, but who siphoned it off? And have you forgotten what Dr Sue eventually admitted after Foster died?"

"That she gave him a lift to the meeting! We never really pursued that, did we?" said Lovell.

"I have been thinking about it. We took our eye off the ball, probably distracted by Verity suddenly collapsing in the grounds of the cathedral. Matt, can you go and see Dr Sue? And I think Jade and I should follow up with Dr Mark, if only for completeness. We can't afford to leave any stone unturned. I think we do need to complete that sticker album, actually.

"Matt, didn't you report that Poppy was a patient of his? Might it be worth our while asking him about it, see if he reacts?"

"I assume you are getting pressure from above?" asked Lovell.

"Yes, Matt, I am. The chief constable is breathing down my neck, but, and this may be divine intervention, the media have been slow to make the link between membership of Glug, Glug and the murders."

"And long may it continue. I would have thought that one of the members might have spilled the beans to a pushy journalist."

"I don't think so. They all still have questions to answer, so why draw more attention to their possible involvement."

Jade spoke up. "I'm amazed that Julie Stringer hasn't put two and two together."

Lovell smiled. "Have you seen her latest column? She is finally losing the plot, I reckon. Some idiot complaining because he ordered 'Death by Chocolate' and yet he is still alive."

"I think it was 'Heart Attack on a Plate'," said Tagg.

"I'd heard that she's got a new man, one of the instructors at Minster Fitness," said Jade.

"Well, whatever or whoever is distracting her, thank God for small mercies. And BBC Searchlight's beam seems to be switched off, but that is probably down to John Tedesco.

He can use his sister Nicky to calm down any speculation," added Lovell.

"Yeah, but the battalions of keyboard warriors will be marching soon enough. Let's call on the doctors and then see where we are. And can one of you visit Smedley at the cathedral? Let's not forget that he wasn't invited to Jackson's drinks party either."

"And neither were the three victims. I'll pop over this morning, check that he's OK."

"Thanks, Matt. And do feel free to carry a pomander."

Various thoughts had been nagging away at Tagg in the early hours. Could the husband have done it? And how much did they really know about Peter and Poppy LaGarde?

Pete had been operating as a seedy timeshare tout under another assumed name just a few years ago. Where did the wealth really come from?

A few Google searches gave her a clue. Poppy's late father was Tiny Herman. She vaguely recognised the name and searched against him. Of course, Herman was the man behind Cockney Coffins.

Tagg had read about them in *Private Eye*. They had acquired, by allegedly underhand means, several small but well-established funeral directors in South East London and had amalgamated them under the Cockney Coffins umbrella, which continued to expand by aggressive acquisition of undertakers' firms from all over outer London.

The *Eye* had uncovered multiple allegations of mis-selling of spurious funeral plans and gleefully exposed details of the lavish lifestyle enjoyed by Herman and his family.

LaGarde boasted about the 'no expenses spared' funeral that had been arranged for his late wife. "Let me hazard a guess as to who the funeral directors might be," Tagg wondered aloud.

If Poppy had left her estate to her husband and the estate included assets from the mighty Herman empire, then LaGarde had motive.

*

Lovell checked in with the Woolford Medical Practice. Dr Sue could spare him some time after morning surgery, so he decided to fill the gap in his schedule by calling in on Martin Smedley.

Production of his warrant card eased him past the officious-looking dragon at the cathedral's admissions desk, then he asked a helpful guide for directions to the archive. He needn't have bothered. He soon realised that it was simply a matter of following his nose.

Smedley smiled at his guest as if all was well, but Lovell quickly sensed that it wasn't.

Trying not to gag in the confined space, he was beyond relieved when Smedley suggested that they find a bench in the cloisters.

"I'm actually rather pleased that you called this morning, Detective Sergeant," he said, once they had located a vacant seat.

He reached into the pocket of his orange corduroy jacket and produced a clump of bubble wrap.

Intrigued, Lovell awaited the explanation.

"I think I may have just received a death threat," said Martin. "I brought it in this morning. I was going to contact Mr Tedesco to see what he would do, and then, by providence, you arrived."

"I see. Do I take it that the threat was in written form? And is it contained in the bubble wrap?"

Martin dug into his other pocket and pulled out a pair of thin cotton gloves.

"We use these for when we touch old manuscripts and so on."

He then proceeded to untangle the bubble wrap, revealing a neatly folded sheet of A4.

He opened it carefully. The message was short and to the point.

'WHIFFY. YOU ARE NEXT.'

"Martin," said Lovell, gently, kindly, "this must have been a huge shock. How was this delivered to you?"

"It was shoved under my door. I saw it when I got home last night. I couldn't sleep, I kept imagining there were people outside. I thought I heard someone throwing stones at my window."

"You poor chap. Have you any idea who would do this?"

"There is only one person who calls me 'Whiffy' – Sylvia Spraggon."

THIRTY-EIGHT

Glug, Glug: Are All the Members Safe?

As he left the cathedral precincts, having done his best to reassure Martin Smedley that he would be protected, Matt Lovell faced a dilemma. Should he go straight to Sylvia Spraggon's house in St Budeaux Place and confront her with the evidence, or should he keep his appointment with Dr Sue?

As time was short, he opted for the latter course of action. He pulled in opposite the Pelistry, the residence of the Master of Musick, and called Tagg, who was being driven by Jade Sennen.

She picked up on the hands-free.

Matt explained about the death threat to Martin and Tagg immediately ordered Jade to turn around when safe and head back to Rhyminster. The plan was that they were going to surprise Dr Mark at home – his secretary had told Jade that he was working on paperwork that day – so they could call in on Sylvia before heading out to the doctors' house in Upper Woolford, the posh bit.

There were no viable spaces available in St Budeaux Place, so Tagg told Jade to park in the Close, finding a space that was outside the eyeline of Cyril the parking officer, who controlled the movement of vehicles from his kiosk at the Broad Street Gate. He was a miserable old git at the best of times and Tagg could do without an argument with him this morning.

When they turned into the mews, Jade saw a light on in the Spraggon residence and Sylvia answered on the third ring.

"Oh joy, it's the keystone cops! I thought I heard the Klaxon coming from the clown car. Thank you interrupting my bowel vacation! This had better be important. Have you arrested LaGarde yet? It's always the husband," she told them with absolute certainty.

"Ms Spraggon," Jade began.

DCI Tagg interrupted, sensing an imminent explosion of anti-woke outrage. "Miss Spraggon," she said with added emphasis. "We do need to share something with you, so please can we continue this conversation inside?"

After brushing away the debris from the sofa with the back of her hand, Sylvia beckoned the officers to take a seat.

"So, what have you pair of cretins got to share with me today? Covid, HIV?"

Tagg controlled herself. This woman was one of the most irritating people she had ever met and that was a high bar to clear.

"Miss Spraggon. What we are about to share with you is highly confidential. It concerns a fellow member of Glug, Glug. Martin Smedley."

Sylvia started to laugh. "So what's old Whiffy been up to?"

*

Matt Lovell pulled into the car park opposite the Woolford Medical Practice with ten minutes to spare, which allowed the dapper DS time to check in the mirror, comb his hair, straighten his tie and go over his line of questioning.

He was ushered into Dr Sue's consulting room. She seemed to have just finished a sandwich lunch, and there was a sudoku puzzle to the side of the lunch remnants.

"Just grabbed a quick bite before our appointment. Sorry about the mess."

"No problem at all. I appreciate your time. We are seeing all the members of your wine club—"

"Are we all suspects?"

Lovell smiled. "You will have noticed, of course, that three members have died in mysterious circumstances. Now, this may be coincidence, but—"

"I don't see how it can be."

"Very well, Dr Elphick. In any case, we need to ask if you are feeling worried about your own safety. Have you received any threats, or noticed any strange cars near your home, or at the surgery?"

"I haven't felt in any danger. I've been too busy with my patients to think about the deaths in any forensic way – but now you've brought it up, should I be worried? And Mark – are you going to see him?"

"One of my colleagues is calling on him, don't worry."

After advising her to be vigilant and to report anything suspicious, Lovell's eye was drawn to a printout which appeared to be a funeral notice.

Dr Sue handed it to him.

"I just printed this before you arrived. It's about poor Poppy's funeral. I think we ought to try and go."

"Could I take a picture of it, do you think?"

The somewhat showy notice revealed that the funeral directors were a firm called Cockney Coffins.

Lovell took a shot of it.

"Is there anything I can help you with?" asked Dr Sue.

"There might be. I think you gave Commander Foster a lift to the last Glug, Glug meeting?"

"I did, yes."

"You weren't so certain about it when you were asked about it earlier. You denied it at first, as I recall."

Her professional mask almost visibly slipped.

"I knew that I wouldn't have time to go home before the tasting; I was meeting a consultant at Rhyminster General. As the Commander lived on the way to the hall, I decided to offer him a lift. There was another reason behind this. He was my patient, and I was quite worried about him. You may have heard, he had fallen out with the cathedral and was no longer the head sidesman. I had asked Martin Smedley to look out for him and Martin had told me that the Commander's house was getting untidy, despite the fact that he employed a cleaner one day a week, and that he was getting confused. So I thought I would see for myself."

"So you were being an old-fashioned GP? There aren't many of those left."

Dr Sue gave a weary shrug. "We all do our best."

"Dr Elphick, this may seem a strange question, but did you notice whether there was a bottle of wine opened at Foster's place? Madeira maybe?"

The doctor hesitated. "No, I don't think so."

"And would you have given him a bottle as a present?"

She replied, rather too quickly perhaps, that of course she hadn't. This would have been highly unprofessional.

As she spoke, Dr Sue tried to remember what she had done with the awful bottle of Madeira that Greville Jackson had foisted on her after his drinks party.

Could she have given it to Foster?

*

Back in Rhyminster, DCI Tagg told Sylvia about the note that had been delivered to Martin Smedley.

"I have to ask you about this, Miss Spraggon. You have just referred to him as 'Whiffy', which was how the note was addressed."

"Well he is whiffy! Have you met him? Human sewage works!"

Tagg ignored the outburst. "The point I was making is that you habitually refer to him by that name. I gather that others in the group have a different way of referring to him."

"Yes. Martin Smelly. I prefer to call him Whiffy. So bloody what. Hang on, you are not suggesting for a moment…"

Jade Sennen, cued in by her boss, asked Sylvia where she had been last night.

"At the fleapit."

"Could you be more specific?"

"The Rhyminster branch of the Odeon. I went with my niece, Demelza. She's doing her houseman year at the General, so I take her out and about. Show her some culture, make sure she's eating."

"And do you remember what the film was?"

"Do you think I've got dementia, you silly girl? Of course I remember. It was horror night. *The Texas Chain Saw Massacre*. I enjoyed it hugely. Not sure Demelza did, but there we are."

"And where were you this morning?"

"Went for a yomp. Round the Close. Always do it. Oils the joints, keeps me regular. No need for a ghastly gym or lesbo tea."

"And what time did you set off on your yomp?"

"It coincides with *Thought for the Day*." Sensing puzzlement, she went on. "Don't you listen to Radio 4? 'Course not. You are young, get all your news from Tic Tac or whatever it's called. *Thought for the Day* is the Radio 4 God talk at about 7.50am. Sends me outside quicker than a dose of salts. Drippy pinko clergy rabbiting on about the third world!"

DCI Tagg shot a knowing look at her junior colleague before speaking to Sylvia.

"So you could have called in at the cathedral then?"

"And maybe delivered a message to someone?" Jade added.

Sylvia looked uncharacteristically worried for a moment.

"Of course I didn't call at the cathedral! What a ridiculous idea!"

As they drove away from Rhyminster, Tagg asked Sennen what she made of the interview with Sylvia.

"I deliberately lobbed in the suggestion that she might have dropped off a message at the cathedral."

"Knowing full well that the message was delivered to Smedley at his home last night. Very clever. And she almost put her foot in it, I reckon. She was hesitating before she replied."

"So shall I check out her alibi?"

"Good call. Dr Demelza should be easy to track down."

THIRTY-NINE

Tedesco and Barker Take a Walk, and Dr Michael Gets a Visit

While the police were out interviewing the remaining members of Glug, Glug, Tedesco had taken a rare day off, leaving Jos to mind the shop with Sally.

It was the quintessential day for a stroll with Barker, sunny and cold, and so the two of them set off in the Lancia. Tedesco had lined up 'No Particular Place to Go' as the musical accompaniment, as he had no specific destination in mind.

"What do you fancy, Barker? Some moorland majesty or some sea air?"

Interpreting the border terrier's lack of a discernible response as licence to choose for both of them, Tedesco turned off the main road and headed towards the nearest beach.

It was practically deserted at this time of year, but the little café was still open, so he got a takeaway coffee and then he released Barker into the wild.

His canine friend seemed thrilled to be back on the ocean's edge. Tedesco congratulated himself on making the correct call and on remembering to pack Barker's beach towel, which came in Plymouth Argyle green, embossed with the words 'I'm a midfield terrier'.

The sea air was aiding the private detective's thought processes. Poirot had his little grey cells; Tedesco thrived on a regular dose of ozone.

The next meeting of Glug, Glug, the last one before Christmas, was only days away. He was coming to a tentative conclusion about the murders but would need to consult Julia Tagg again, once she and her team had visited all of the members.

There were practical steps to consider. As he hurled the yellow tennis ball for Barker to chase into the waves, he had something of a brainwave.

Woolford Village Hall, where the wine club held its meetings, was the usual venue for wakes held after funerals in the parish church or the nearby crematorium. Did they live-stream them? This practice had become very common during the pandemic, when numbers were restricted, and had continued as a means of enabling far-flung relatives to attend the funeral and any subsequent gathering virtually and still, somehow, feel part of the gathering.

He would get in touch with old Stander, the caretaker. He'd know all about it.

If this came off, then the police could watch the proceedings remotely and then join the gluggers in person when he had unveiled the murderer. His current thinking suggested that it was a single individual rather than a group, although there was still room for doubt. There was always room for doubt, whether in matters of crime or matters of faith.

*

As Tedesco was enjoying his therapeutic break with Barker, DCI Julia Tagg and DC Jade Sennen were sitting in Dr Mark Elphick's study in Woolford.

"I didn't know that GPs worked from home. I assumed you had to be in the surgery all the time," said Jade.

Dr Mark smiled – kindly, thought the DC. Or at least not unkindly.

"And I thought you all spent all your time at the station. Actually, we can work remotely these days. A lot of my consultations are carried out over the internet, or the phone, and I can log in to the practice from here. Of course, it helps that I am married to the senior partner! She is hardly likely to turn down my requests for flexible working, is she?"

DCI Tagg took note of Dr Mark's reference to his wife's seniority in the practice – did she detect a hint of something there? Jealousy perhaps, or bitterness?

She decided to crack on.

"Dr Elphick. Firstly, thank you for seeing us today. You are probably wondering why we are here."

The GP shifted in his seat. "I assume it's about the murders. We are all in regular contact – the members of Glug, Glug, that is – so I know that everyone is being interviewed."

"To put your mind at rest, this isn't a formal interview," Julia said, reassuringly.

"That's right," added Jade. "We wanted to check how you all are. Three of your group have been killed so we are asking if you have felt frightened, or noticed anything suspicious, such as strangers hanging around near your home or the surgery."

Dr Mark thought for a moment. "No, nothing specific. But we – Sue and I – have become much more careful about security, forever checking that we have set the alarms and so on."

Then DCI Tagg threw her protégé a knowing look, as if to cue her in.

DC Sennen took a deep breath before asking the next question.

"Dr Elphick, can you confirm whether the late Poppy LaGarde was one of your patients?"

The doctor was momentarily lost for words.

"Look," said Julia Tagg, "if you are worried about patient confidentiality, it may help if I tell you that Peter LaGarde told us that you were his late wife's GP."

Dr Mark broke his temporary silence. "You are right. I didn't want to breach confidentiality, but if Peter has told you that I was Poppy's doctor, then I am not going to deny it. But I cannot and will not discuss her records."

"We weren't asking you to, Dr Elphick," Jade said.

"But we can obtain them if we have to," added Julia, instantly wondering if this had sounded a bit aggressive.

"Why are you asking me about Poppy anyway?"

"You sound a bit defensive, if you don't mind me saying."

"No I don't! Look here, are you suggesting that I had anything to do with her death?"

Tagg tried to take the temperature down a notch.

"No, of course not. I apologise if that is how it came out."

"Poppy was the last person I would wish to harm. She was a very good person, you know. She raised a fortune for the Wishing Well appeal."

Tagg knew about the appeal. The local great and good had formed the charity to raise money for the hospital and this funded stuff that the NHS couldn't afford, like a new MRI scanner. Tedesco's PA, Sally, was a regular participant in the annual Walk for the Wards and had persuaded her to join in this time.

Although the comprehensive-school-educated DCI maintained an instinctive scepticism towards upper-class philanthropy – why couldn't they just pay their fair share of tax? – she had to concede that the Wishing Well appeal had done amazingly well, and that the hospital would struggle without it.

She signalled to Jade that the meeting was coming to an end and they both stood up.

"We will find our own way out. And please get in touch if you see or hear anything worrying or suspicious."

"Could I just ask – are you any closer to finding out who is behind all this?"

Tagg looked the doctor straight in the eye. "I think we might be, Dr Mark."

As they drove back towards Rhyminster, Tagg suggested that she drop Sennen off at the General, so that she could check if Sylvia's niece was working. Jade could walk back to the nick from there in five minutes.

"So, pick the bones out of that one, DC Sennen!"

"He seemed very protective about Poppy, I thought."

"Good, notice anything else?"

"He seemed a bit uncomfortable when he mentioned his wife – that comment about needing her permission to work from home. It was one of those jokes that wasn't really a joke, if that makes sense."

"Oh yes, DC Sennen. It makes perfect sense."

*

"You can have five minutes. I need to be back on the ward…"

"I can imagine. Dr Spraggon, you are probably wondering why a detective has called in to interrupt your busy day."

"Please call me Demelza. My aunt had warned me that you might be asking me to confirm where I was last night."

"And where were you?"

"At the cinema with Aunt Sylvia. She took me to see a dreadful film, *The Texas Chain Saw Massacre*. We went to the 6pm screening."

"And can you prove it?"

Demelza produced her phone. "Look – here are the e-tickets."

Sennen had a peek, and then she asked the doctor why she had obtained the tickets. "I thought that your aunt was taking you out?"

Demelza laughed. "Have you met Sylvia? She hates the fact that you can only book online. She comes up with the film or whatever but relies on me to get the tickets. She does pay me back, in cash of course, and we go out to supper afterwards."

"What time did you go home?"

"About 10pm, I think. I gave her a lift back to St Budeaux Place."

Sennen smiled. "Your aunt is quite a character."

"Infuriating, force of nature, but she has a heart of gold. I've been glad of her company, moving to a new city. Now, I really must get back to work."

Having thanked Demelza for her help, Sennen set off for

the station, satisfied that Sylvia had her alibi. But if she hadn't slipped the note – 'WHIFFY. YOU ARE NEXT.' – under Martin Smedley's door, then who had?

FORTY

Tedesco and Tagg Hatch a Plan

"DCI Tagg! I was going to call you."

"Great minds think alike. I think it's time we met up again, don't you?"

After bumping into Dr Sue and Dr Mark at their last meeting at the Kingfisher, they agreed to meet at Tedesco's place for a catch-up after supper. No chance of being overheard there, except by Barker. And he was the soul of discretion.

Jools took no time in updating her friend and fellow detective on the recent key developments in the case. Tedesco took notes as she told him about the 'Whiffy note' and Sylvia's alibi, the link between Cockney Coffins, the Herman family and Peter LaGarde, and Dr Sue's rather unconvincing explanation for offering Foster a lift to the wine tasting.

He raised a quizzical eyebrow when he heard that Poppy had been a patient of Dr Mark and looked up when he heard about how the doctor might have given away that he felt an element of jealousy when it came to his wife's position as senior partner.

"That could be significant. Jos told me that Sue looked 'winded' when she called in to see him. But what do you think? Are you any closer to an arrest? Are the deaths linked? I know that it looked that way, but…"

DCI Tagg puffed out her cheeks and then she said, "Did you notice that I walked over this evening?"

"So you can join me in a drink! I've got a bottle of red open. It's a Malbec, quite fruity, decent finish."

"It sounds wonderful, thanks."

While Tedesco poured the wine, Barker appeared and tapped Jools gently on the leg with his outstretched paw.

"Hello, Barker! Have you got any idea who our suspect might be?"

Barker curled up under the DCI's chair to have a good think about it.

Jools took a generous sip, and then she replied to Tedesco's burst of questioning.

"To answer your questions, we aren't any closer to an arrest. Every time we sense a breakthrough, something else clouds the picture. And honestly, I haven't a clue whether it's one of the gluggers, several of them, or whether the whole group will have bumped each other off before we get to the bottom of it. And I can feel the pressure from above, as well as from the surviving members."

Tedesco decided that now was the time to remind her about his plan to smoke out the killer, or killers, by using the next Glug, Glug meeting as a chance to discuss what had happened while serving the wines.

"So what are you suggesting? You interrogate them all and then reveal the murderer? Like Cluedo?"

"I was taking my inspiration from Agatha Christie, actually," he said, sounding a bit wounded. "But don't you see?" he insisted. "They will all be in the same room, they will have been drinking, so I could trip one or more of them up. It's worth a go, surely?"

"Pour me another glass of that red and I'll have a think about it."

As they steadily worked their way down the bottle, Jools had to admit that she had nothing to lose from Tedesco's initiative.

"It's in three days' time. I've spoken to the caretaker, and they do have recording facilities, so I can send you the Zoom link and you can log in at the station. If I get a confession then you can come over and make an arrest."

"Hmm. This is a total long shot. I must need my head examining, but let's go for it. John, can I put you on the spot? Do you have any idea who done it?"

"I do have an idea and will need to use the next few days to add what you told me tonight into my case notes, but using my little grey cells…"

"I think it's time for me to go now, don't you? Barker, make sure he gets a good night's sleep and doesn't stay up all night listening to his sad songs by old men."

"I can tell that you've been spending time with Lynne! Safe home."

Then his phone rang, the loud ringtone startling Barker.

"I know you hate it, but it's the Argyle anthem! Tedesco! This had better be important," he told the late-night caller.

It was. When he put the phone down a few minutes later, Tedesco was grinning from ear to ear.

"We are going to be having a surprise guest, Barker, and I think you will get on very well."

FORTY-ONE

Time to Involve Jos

The next morning, Barker was momentarily taken aback by his master's sprightly start to the day.

"Come on, Barker, we need to get in early, lots to do."

Barker had heard it all before, and as he knew that he could have a nap once they got to the office, he was prepared to tolerate this latest burst of unexpected enthusiasm.

"I'll call Sandra and see if she can do a few more hours this week, as we need to make up the spare room. And then I need to bring Jos up to speed."

Sandra was the legendary cleaner to, among others, the bishop and Lady Derrington, but as she had been the cleaner at Tedesco's old law firm before she reached her current status, mainly through his contact book, she was always happy to give him priority. And she had a huge crush on Barker.

Once they had made it through the Cathedral Close and up the helter-skelter staircase, Tedesco dropped Barker off at 4A Minster Precincts then went up to the next floor, 4B, to see if Jos was around.

The door was open, and the detective was rewarded with

the sight of his friend struggling to slit open a huge delivery box.

"Knock, knock. Can I help?"

"John! Could you just hold the box steady for me? That's it, I can get some purchase on it now."

Once the box was opened, Jos pulled out a bottle of Côtes du Rhône and presented it to his colleague in the informal 'Crime and Wine' alliance.

"Something for later. As ever, I'd value your opinion."

"And, as ever, it will be an absolute pleasure to give it. Actually, this isn't entirely a social call."

Jos appeared anxious. "Is it more bad news?"

"No, no. It's about the next tasting."

"I had wondered if it was going to happen, to be honest, but I spoke to Dr Sue earlier and she said that all the members – the survivors – are determined to carry on as normal."

"The Blitz spirit is alive and well in deepest Devon, then."

"Seems like it. I was going to pop down and see you later. I don't have a theme for this tasting, and it's only two days away."

"Why not call it a mystery tasting? That leaves open a range of possibilities."

"A mystery tasting it is! Thanks, John."

"It was Barker's idea. Actually, what I wanted to talk about was how we structure the evening. I have a plan and want to see if you are alright with it. Why don't we meet in a corner of the refectory in about an hour?"

Tedesco went back to his office and answered a few emails. He wasn't as busy as he used to be but had another promising – and potentially lucrative – cheating couple case involving two high-profile local characters, and he was being chased up by his client on a daily basis.

Jos busied himself with his order book and before they both knew it, it was time to head across the green to the refectory.

The wine merchant made it first and secured a table in an alcove which was out of sight of the tourists.

Jos had ordered their usual – a pot of Minster Blend tea, of course – and after a polite tussle over who would be mother, Tedesco outlined his plan.

"You say that DCI Tagg is alright about it? And that the hall has recording facilities?"

"Oh yes, and a gas boiler and everything." Tedesco was always amused at how unworldly his colleague could be as he explained, to Jos's bewilderment, the concept of live-streaming funerals.

"But will I be treated as a suspect as well?"

"Yes. I will go through everyone in the room, setting out their possible motive before I reveal the truth."

"You seem very certain!"

"I need to spend tomorrow at home going through my case notes again. Jools has given me some new information that I need to feed in, but I haven't changed my mind yet. And I have a visitor, someone in my line of work."

"And is this person coming to the tasting?"

"Oh yes. This person knows quite a bit about wine – well, fortified wine."

"Madeira?"

"Wait and see."

Their tête-á-tête was briefly interrupted by an impromptu pastoral visit from Canon Wilfred, asking how they both were.

Once the kindly priest had scurried off back into the cathedral, Jos announced that he had an idea.

"Why don't we link the wines we taste to each of the suspects?"

"I like it. So we taste a bottle of Stonker – Sylvia; a bottle of the white that allegedly poisoned Poppy LaGarde…"

"And, although I have my reputation to consider, we will have to include a bottle of the ghastly Madeira! Leave this part to me, John. I think it might be quite fun, in a morbid sort of way."

"I knew I could rely on you, old friend. Could you do me another favour? As I said, I need to work at home tomorrow, so could you mind the shop for me?"

DCI Tagg and DS Matt Lovell attended the funeral of Poppy LaGarde in London that afternoon. They could both have done without it, but the chief constable was tied up and wanted the force to be represented.

Describing the experience to Tedesco when she returned to Rhyminster, Jools reported that the ceremony had been somewhat tacky.

"You would have absolutely hated it. It was like something out of *Eastenders*, or the Kray Twins movie. There were no hymns, unless you include 'My Way', 'Angels' and 'The One and Only'."

"It does sound dreadful, but if it provided comfort, who are we to sneer? Anyway, did you manage to talk to Peter?"

"Matt did. He said it was like getting blood out of a particularly pissed-off stone. But LaGarde did confirm that he would be at the wine tasting. He wouldn't miss it for the world, apparently."

FORTY-TWO

A Day to Reflect, and a Guest Arrives

Tedesco was up early for his walk around the Close with Barker, surprising the border terrier by returning home in a circular route rather than continuing across Cathedral Green to the office.

Once back in the snug confines of St Budeaux Place, he boiled a kettle and made a large cafetière of coffee, which he took up to his study. He remained there for the rest of the day, stopping only to check on the dog.

He felt a bit like the Chancellor of the Exchequer on the eve of the budget. Instead of frantically checking that his figures stacked up, he was going through his immaculate case notes. He had drawn up a kind of family tree with branches going off in different directions, but instead of family members, this tree contained the names of the surviving gluggers.

As he checked and rechecked, he was more certain of his methodology than ever and that the conclusion he had reached, namely that one individual was responsible for the three murders, was watertight.

The mystery tasting could not come soon enough. This killer could strike again.

Later that afternoon, while Tedesco was framing questions to raise at the meeting, a large, black, electric car sporting two pennants swept off Broad Street and turned into the road leading to the outer Cathedral Close, causing the dawdling tourists to leap back onto the pavement in terror.

As the driver approached the kiosk, Cyril the traffic manager came out and put up his hand in the universally understood 'Halt!' gesture.

The driver, dressed in full chauffeur's uniform, leaned out of the driver's side window, looking surprised to be stopped.

"Where do you think you are going, mate?" said Cyril.

The chauffeur shrugged.

"You can't drive through unless you have business with the bishop or the dean. Which is it?"

"*O quê?*"

"Foreign, eh? No speak English?"

Cyril was suddenly aware of the passenger, a tall man dressed in back and wearing dark glasses.

The man exited the car and moved towards the elderly traffic warden, decisively but unthreateningly.

"Let me explain. Francisco has a somewhat limited command of English. What you need to understand, my friend, is that he works for the Portuguese Ambassador to the Court of St James's. Have you clocked the flags?"

"I wondered what they were, yeah. But you still can't just drive into the Close."

"I am on ambassadorial business, so I think I can."

"Not having it. And it gets right under my skin when someone I don't know calls me 'my friend'."

"What would you rather I called you? *Gringo*? *Amigo*? English?"

"Now you are just taking the Michael. I suggest you tell Ronaldo here to turn round and get out of town."

"I don't think so, *amigo*. Now, you don't want to cause an international incident with this country's oldest ally, do you? Let us through. I don't want to keep Mr Tedesco waiting."

"Are you staying with John and Barker? He said he was having an important guest. Why didn't you say? Just drive around the Close following the arrows, then through the south gate. His place is on the left."

As Francisco drove under the uplifted barrier, Tony Camacho leaned out of the window and waved at Cyril.

"*Tchau, gringo.*"

The arrival of the black Mercedes in the tiny mews alerted Tedesco's fierce guard dog. Barker ran up the stairs and barked at his master.

"What is it? You don't want another walk already?"

Barker did his best to convey 'It's behind you!' in mime and Tedesco went to the window.

"It must be Tony! Come on, Barker, let's welcome our guest!"

Tony, travelling light, dropped his expensive-looking leather travel bag, in black of course, in the porch and shook hands firmly with his host, who urged him over the threshold.

Barker, a little starstruck, wandered up to this new human acquaintance somewhat gingerly.

Tony bent down – no mean feat for such a tall man – and stroked the border terrier. "Barker! We meet at last. An absolute pleasure."

The little dog wandered off, tail wagging merrily as he retreated to the warmth of his basket.

Tedesco gave his fellow sleuth the guided tour, which

took all of five minutes, then he served his guest his best coffee.

"I have a gift for you. From the ambassador. I was staying at the residence in London last night."

"Ah, so that explains the official car. I bet that caused a stir in the Close. Is he a friend of yours, the ambassador?"

"She is, yes. We go way back."

Tedesco decided that 'no further questions, Your Honour' was the correct approach, so he turned the conversation to Funchal, asking after Lita and Reggie Challenor.

"The bar is still going well, as is our little arrangement. Lita sends her love. And Sir Reggie is in fine form. He sent you a gift as well."

Tony retrieved his bag and pulled out a beautifully gift-wrapped present, clearly a bottle, and a tie.

The tie, bearing the Challenor family crest and a motto which Tony told him meant 'Don't let the bastards get you down' in medieval French, was obviously from Sir Reggie and the other present was a bottle of vintage port, which came with an official-looking card which offered the compliments of the ambassador.

"I'm overwhelmed," said Tedesco, suggesting, a little unwisely, that they might uncork the port later that evening. "I thought a walk to a country pub might be in order," he proposed.

"I can't think of anything better, as long as they serve wine. I draw the line at your warm beer."

FORTY-THREE

From Funchal to Rhyminster

Tony was charmed by the views of the cathedral as they walked through the water meadows to the Kingfisher.

"I understand why you have stayed here for so long, John. I could imagine retiring to somewhere like this."

Resisting the temptation to remind his guest that he was not retired, far from it, Tedesco warned Tony to duck when they entered the old inn.

"I see what you mean! They must have been tiny in those days."

Tedesco, mindful of Tony's comment about warm beer, ordered a couple of ice-cold lagers.

"So," he opened the conversation, "what were you doing at the embassy?"

"Cheers, John! Great to be here. Listen, I'm not just Funchal's gentleman extraordinaire, you know. I have a side hustle as an international man of mystery. But the visit was well timed, as I could call in on you before I fly back."

Tedesco gave a sly little smile and then took a sip of his beer. "It could be very well timed indeed."

He then proceeded to explain about the wine society, the

murders – lowering his voice as he did so – and the plan to expose the perpetrator.

They broke to discuss the menu, deciding to share a whole baked brill and to match it with a bottle of white.

Tony scoured the wine list.

"Great, they have a Portuguese wine here. Firnão Pires grape variety, known as Maria Gomes in Bairrada."

Tedesco broke out into a broad grin. "I didn't know you were such an expert, but I can't pretend to be surprised. Could you help us out at the tasting tomorrow?"

"It would be an honour."

*

When they got back, Tedesco declined the suggestion that they sample the ambassador's port, as he needed to have his wits about him for the next day.

"I hope the spare room is alright, Tony. It might be a bit of a squeeze!"

Barker obviously thought that Tony was a pretty cool dude for a human, as he followed him upstairs and maintained an overnight guard outside his room.

FORTY-FOUR

The Day of the Tasting

Tony was already up and about when Tedesco surfaced at 7.30am. He had helped himself to coffee and was stroking Barker when his host asked him about breakfast.

"Can we eat out somewhere? My treat."

"That's very kind of you, but Rhyminster doesn't have the variety of cafés that you have in Madeira."

"But you have somewhere which does bacon sarnies?"

Tedesco thought for a moment. "We do! The Greedy Pig! It's in the market square, it's been around since before I moved here, and it is dog-friendly. Let's go there first, then I'll introduce you to Jos Elsted, who is the wine side of the business."

As the three of them wandered through the Close, Tony asked if he could visit the cathedral while Tedesco was working.

"Of course! I will need to catch up after working from home yesterday, so why don't you wander back over here once I have shown you the office."

"Ah, the famous Minster Precincts! This is like visiting Baker Street with Sherlock Holmes!"

"Well, I suppose Jos might fit the role of Watson, but my PA is hardly Mrs Hudson, as you will soon discover."

Tony drew interested glances from the citizens of Rhyminster as they made their way down Broad Street and into the square.

The Greedy Pig had opened early for market day, and the place was already full, so they had to sit outside.

"This is great, John. You can watch the world go by, just like in Funchal."

"The weather isn't so great, though," said Tedesco, stifling a sneeze.

The waiter recognised Barker and brought him some water in a special dog bowl bearing a red paw print, then he took the order for two greedy bacon specials and some more coffee.

The bacon sarnies were delicious, made with the café's home-made sourdough and slathered in butter from Rhyme Dairies.

Tony went inside to pay the bill, which seemed to take an age.

He emerged with the business card of the manager.

Sensing Tedesco's puzzlement, he explained that he had asked to see the owner, and they swapped cards.

"I can picture this in Funchal. A Greedy Pig branch, a joint venture, marketed at the locals and the hordes of Brits we host every year. I will touch base with Fergus when I get back."

"I have to hand it to you, Tony – every day is a business opportunity for someone like you."

"And it can be for you, my friend. Let's have a look at the famous agency!"

As they made their way up the spiral staircase to Tedesco's office, Jos Elsted, looking like a human version of Paddington Bear in his duffel coat, was heading back downstairs.

"John! I don't suppose you and your guest can help me with the deliveries."

Tony stepped forward and introduced himself. "Sure, lead on!"

While the three wine aficionados busied themselves with the cases of wine for that evening's tasting, Barker trotted up to the office and barked outside the door, which alerted Sally.

"Hello, Barker! On your own today?"

The border terrier gave Sally a somewhat withering look as she let him in, and then he made straight for his 'work' basket under Tedesco's desk.

Once the cases had been taken up to 4B, Tedesco led Tony and Jos back down to 4A. Sally gave her best impression of a Victorian heroine having an attack of the vapours when she was introduced to the tall, dark stranger, then she scuttled off to make some coffee while her boss showed his guests into the little interview room before completing the formal introductions.

"Tony, meet Jos Elsted; Jos, this is Tony Camacho. We met in Madeira."

"Of course!" said Jos. "John has told me all about you."

"All true, I fear. And John has filled me in about your wine business. Now, I know all about tonight, but perhaps we could stay in touch once the culprit is revealed? I have excellent contacts in the wine trade."

Sensing a slight unease from his friend and colleague, who probably hadn't dealt with anyone quite as direct as Tony before, Tedesco explained to Jos that Tony really did know his wines and that he would have an invaluable role to play in the upcoming meeting of Glug, Glug.

"What did you have in mind?" asked Tony, in his smooth mid-Atlantic tones.

Tedesco paused to allow Sally, still transfixed by Tony, to deposit the coffee and pastries, fresh that morning from Jenks Bakery.

"Jos, as I think I explained to you, Tony here has already come across two of the members in Madeira."

Tony chipped in. "Yeah, an eccentric old dear and a conman."

Jos smiled nervously. "Do I assume that you are referring to Sylvia Spraggon and Peter LaGarde?"

"He went by the name of Fairfax when I knew him," Tony replied. "He was ripping off gullible Brits in a timeshare scam."

"Gosh," said Jos.

Tedesco explained that he would like Tony to wait in an anteroom with the caretaker, Stander, who would be dealing with the live-streaming, and then he would go and fetch him at the appropriate time.

"Tony, depending on how things pan out, I expect the best moment for you to make your entrance might be while I am cross-examining Peter LaGarde."

"How exciting. That would be a real coup du théâtre!" said Jos, whose mood had improved somewhat.

Tedesco knew that his friend had reason to fear the coming evening, as he would be treated as a suspect like everyone else there and would be open to attack from the likes of LaGarde, but it seemed that the surprise addition of the man from Funchal to the mix had lifted his spirits.

Tony was the next to speak.

"The wines – will they include Madeira? You don't expect me to extol its virtues, do you?"

Tedesco laughed. "I might sneak a bottle in, depends on whether it helps to trap the guilty party, but I am sure you can talk with great authority about a new *vinho verde* that Jos has tracked down."

"It's a real bargain," said Jos. "I'm rather hoping that the members order some bottles after the meeting."

Tedesco, suddenly serious, said that he doubted if anyone would be in the mood to buy wine by the time the tastings were done. Deep down, he wondered if this would be the final tasting; the end of Glug, Glug; down the metaphorical plughole.

Once the plans were finalised, Tony set off for his tour of the cathedral and its environs.

He would meet Tedesco at his place later in the afternoon, and Jos would take the van over to Woolford.

FORTY-FIVE

All Will Be Revealed

There was an expectant buzz in the room as Dr Sue called the meeting to order. It wasn't the type of buzz that one associates with an excited audience as the house lights dim before the entrance of a beloved entertainer: this was more anxious, as if those present were waiting for a guillotine to drop.

Sue went through the formalities with her customary efficiency and Sylvia Spraggon leapt up to question her when she announced that she had received no apologies for absence.

"What about Foster, Verity and Poppy? They are absent."

"But they can hardly send their apologies, can they?" countered Greville Jackson.

Dr Sue explained that she was going to call for a minute's silence before the meeting commenced, in memory of their colleagues, then she signalled to Tedesco to start the tasting.

"Thank you, Madam Secretary. With your agreement, I thought that it might be more appropriate to honour the memory of Thomas, Verity and Poppy by toasting them. After all, it was our love of wine that brought us all together."

Sensing a general murmur of approval, Tedesco signalled for Jos to start pouring the special wine that the two of them had selected for the occasion.

"Jos has found this white Burgundy from a small producer which bears the appropriate name of Memoriam."

"I hope the wine tastes better than the naff name," muttered Sylvia as Jos poured her a generous measure.

Tedesco stood up, glass in hand, to propose the toast.

"Fellow members. Lord Byron said that wine cheers the sad, revives the old, inspires the young and makes weariness forget his toil. With this wine, let us all remember Commander Thomas Foster, Verity Glynde and Poppy LaGarde. To the memory of old friends!"

"To the memory of old friends," echoed the gluggers.

"Now, with your further indulgence, I will hand over to Jos Elsted, our esteemed vintner, who will explain this evening's tasting."

"Thank you, John. We thought that we should do things a little differently tonight. As we have just tasted a wine in memory of our friends, we thought that it would be a nice idea to taste wines that are your particular favourites.

"We have used the markings from previous tastings and my order book to see which wines you all prefer. As this is a special evening, rather than marking the wines, I am going to invite each of you to comment on why you like yours."

"I think that's a champion idea," said retired market gardener Jim Clayton.

"Get on with it, Elsted," Peter LaGarde said, glancing at his ostentatious watch.

"Right! We have drawn your names out of a hat, and Sylvia is first up," Jos announced, while Tedesco circled the room filling fresh glasses with a deep-red wine.

"Sylvia, would you care to start us off? What are we drinking and why do you like it?"

"It's called the Stonker, as I think most you know, and it's from South Africa. And why do I like it? Because it's firm, almost stiff on the tongue, and it has a long, sticky finish."

"And what year is this vintage, 1969?" said Rachel Lowndes.

Tedesco took this ill-judged, snarky comment as his cue to turn the meeting on its head.

"Sylvia. I have a question for you. You have referred to Martin Smedley in the past as 'Whiffy', haven't you?"

She spluttered as she took a gulp of her favourite wine. "What of it?"

Tedesco reached into his coat pocket.

"So did you deliver this note to him?"

He brandished the note and asked Jos to show it to each of the members in turn, finishing with Sylvia. Then he asked her to read it out.

"Bloody ridiculous. Alright then. It says, 'WHIFFY. YOU ARE NEXT.'"

Tedesco paused for effect. "Whiffy. Only you refer to Martin by that name."

"The rest of us call him 'Martin Smelly,'" interjected Stephen Lowndes.

Tedesco continued. "The note was placed under Martin's door. Perhaps you could explain what you meant by stating that he would be next?"

"It was you!" said Peter LaGarde, pointing an accusatory finger at Sylvia. "I was convinced it was Elsted. The old bag is a serial killer!"

"Let Sylvia speak, please," said Tedesco, in his best courtroom manner.

"Of course I didn't write this note. Look, it's in block

capitals. Anyone could have written it. One of you is trying to frame me. Well bloody good luck with that!"

Tedesco spoke calmly. "Sylvia. Could you tell the court – I'm so sorry, the meeting – where you were when the note was delivered last week."

To gasps from Mary Clayton and Rachel Lowndes, Sylvia announced that she had already answered this question when asked by the police.

Tedesco turned to her. "I'm sorry to have put you through that, Sylvia. The police did ask you about the note and you gave them an alibi which checked out."

Jos looked across at his colleague, who raised an eyebrow to cue him in.

"Fellow gluggers, I am afraid that John and I haven't been entirely honest with you. As you all know, we operate as an informal alliance between the wine side of things and John's detective agency."

"So what are you saying, Elsted? Spit it out, man!" shouted Greville Jackson. "I haven't got all night, you know. Smollett will soon be shitting all over the carpet."

"Let me explain, please. The agency has been taking an interest in the three deaths, as you would expect it to. We have now reached the point where John can reveal the murderer."

"Well, it wasn't me or Jim, so let's do it," said Mary Clayton.

"Very clever," said Peter LaGarde, who began to slow hand clap. "So, if any of us kick off, or leave the meeting, it just makes us look guilty."

"Well, are you? Guilty, that is?" asked Sylvia.

Dr Mark, the chairman of Glug, Glug, stood up. "Look, this seems pretty irregular, John. But if you know something, then I for one think that you should share it with us. After all, you aren't the police."

"I agree with Mark," said Rachel Lowndes.

"So do I," said Stephen.

"Shall we let John continue?" asked Dr Mark.

The motion was deemed to be passed by general murmurings and chunterings of consent.

"I need a drink!" said Greville Jackson.

"Right then! The next name we drew out of the hat was Jim Clayton. We have chosen a floral wine that he orders from Jos."

Jos explained that the wine came from the centre of the Beaujolais Crus, and that it was a light and floral red, reflecting the Gamay grape variety.

The atmosphere in the room calmed down somewhat as the members swirled the wine before sipping it, Jackson making his habitual revolting noises as he spat into the spittoon.

"I like this one," said Dr Sue. "I think I might prescribe it to my patients."

"Why do you like it, Jim?" asked Jos.

"It's champion. Silky, if you know what I mean."

"Much nicer than the awful Stonker," muttered Martin Smedley. Despite Sylvia's apparent alibi, he still didn't entirely trust the woman.

Tedesco stood and turned to Jim.

"Ladies and gentlemen, could Jim be involved in any of the murders?"

"Now wait a minute."

"Shut up, Clayton, he's going to go through all of us before he reveals the conclusion," said Rachel.

"Let's think. Jim used to run a garden centre and is still

involved in horticulture. I gather that he helps some of you with advice about plants and so on. And weedkiller."

Jim looked worried as Tedesco asked him if he had ever recommended or ordered a brand called Weed Murderer.

"Aye, what of it?"

"Is this product commercially available?"

"I can get hold of it."

"Have you got a licence?"

Mary tried to help her husband. "Come on, Jim. We have nothing to hide. You told that nice policeman that you ordered it for Rachel."

"Aye, that I did. But some bugger broke into my shed and siphoned some of it off."

"I never ordered it!" said Rachel. "The police know it."

"They asked me about it as well," said Peter LaGarde.

"Anything to add, Mr Jackson?" said Tedesco.

"I never ordered the stuff, if that's what you are thinking?"

"But the police asked you about it, didn't they?" Tedesco turned to the Claytons. "You told the police that you had supplied this substance to Rachel, Peter and Greville. And, Mary, you were convinced that the consignment that was tampered with was ordered by Rachel – or that's what you told the police. So, someone is lying. Oh, and I think I can share this with the group. Weed Murderer contains cyanide in crystal form. And three granules of it were found in the wine that killed Poppy."

Then he paused for effect again, before turning to Jos.

"Next wine, please," he said, in the manner of Professor Chris Whitty calling for the next slide during the pandemic briefings.

Jos brandished a bottle of yellow-coloured wine.

"It's not fucking Madeira, surely?" complained Greville Jackson.

"It looks like a urine sample," said Jim.

"Jim! Really!" said Mary.

"Who the hell likes that cough medicine?" asked Sylvia.

Jos smiled, somewhat uncertainly, knowing what was coming. He had lined up one of the gluggers before the meeting to go along with his ruse.

"Dr Mark, I have no orders for Madeira in my records, and Sue has confirmed that the club has never tasted it. But I remembered that you asked me if I could order some."

The doctor nodded his head. "That's right. My lovely grandmother was partial to it, and so I have always had a taste for Madeira. A bit of a guilty pleasure."

"I think we should sack him as chairman. Madeira indeed!" shouted Greville.

Jos, ignoring the old thespian, explained to the group that John Tedesco had indirectly sourced a rather special batch of Madeira wine and that it was surprisingly effective when served chilled.

Tedesco stood up.

"At this point, I have a guest to introduce. I met him on a recent trip to Funchal, and, by happy coincidence, he is staying with me this week."

Tony, who had been enjoying a smoke and a natter with old Stander in the yard outside the kitchen, quickly stubbed out his cigar and entered the main hall.

"Fellow gluggers, please welcome my friend and fellow investigator, Tony Camacho!"

Tony saluted and then circled the table, presenting each member with one of his cards.

"Gentleman extraordinaire, eh," said Jim Clayton.

Two members of the group appeared to be uncharacteristically sheepish.

Tedesco decided to let Sylvia and Peter LaGarde mull as to where they might have seen the stranger before, and then he asked Tony to introduce the wine, while Jos went around the table pouring it into fresh tasting glasses.

Tony spoke.

"I think I might have overheard some negative comments about the wine of my beautiful island. You may be surprised to learn that I agree – it can taste a bit like cough medicine. But that is your fault, the British, no? You like sweet wines, don't you? When I studied here, the only stuff you drank was Blue Nun. But on the island, we have developed dry varieties. This one is called 'Equerry' after our main backer, Sir Reginald Challenor. I have to declare an interest as a fellow investor.

"It is a limited edition, from a small producer, and so we like to keep it for ourselves. But tonight, you have the opportunity to try it and, I hope, change your mind about Madeira."

"Hmm. Better than the usual gut rot," was the considered opinion of Greville Jackson.

Both Mary Clayton and Rachel Lowndes gave positive reviews, while Sylvia seemed to be more fixated on Tony than she was on the contents of her glass.

"I know where I've seen you before!" she suddenly exclaimed. "It was in Funchal! And you exposed him" – she pointed at Peter LaGarde – "as a timeshare conman. You looked different then, didn't you, Mr Fairfax?"

LaGarde got up. "I've had just about enough of this. And guess what, I'm resigning. You lot know precisely two things about wine: nothing and bugger all. Enjoy your sad little lives; I've got a business to run."

"And a widow to grieve?" asked Stephen Lowndes, more than a little pointedly.

"Sit down, Fairfax, LaGarde or whoever you are tonight. No one is going anywhere," said a suddenly masterful and magnificent Jos. It was as if Paddington Bear had given LaGarde his hardest of hard stares.

"We have all agreed to tonight's format and we haven't heard from everyone yet, have we, John?"

"We certainly haven't heard about your part in this, Elsted," said Peter.

"I've changed my mind again. It was you, wasn't it?" he added, with menace.

Tedesco calmed the meeting by announcing that he was going to turn to Jos as the next suspect.

The wine they would be tasting would be an Italian Barolo, which Jos had chosen as his *Desert Island Wine* in a wine-based podcast based on the long-running Radio 4 programme.

Tony acted as sommelier, and the members all made appreciative sounds as they swirled and sipped. Even Greville Jackson.

Then Tedesco turned to his friend. He wasn't going to treat him gently. For the purposes of this evening, he was just another suspect.

"Fellow members, I have to acknowledge that Jos does have some questions to answer. Firstly, he supplied the wine that contained the granules of cyanide that poisoned Poppy. Next up, the bottles of Madeira found at the scenes of the first two crimes bore the Elsted Wines label."

"That's more like it," shouted Peter.

"Shut up, Fairfax," retorted Sylvia. "Let Elsted defend himself."

Jos stood up, every inch the prisoner in the dock.

"To the first charge, that I supplied the wine for Commander Foster's wake, I stand guilty as charged, but I certainly didn't supply the poison!"

Greville Jackson couldn't help himself. "You've been serving us poison for years, ha ha!"

"Shut up, *Squiffy*!" said Martin Smedley, who won himself a round of applause.

"Do continue," said Tedesco, proud of how well Jos was coping under pressure.

"As for the wine bottles, I must admit that I am puzzled. I have never supplied Madeira, as my books will prove."

Dr Sue stood up. "If it helps, the club records show that we have never ordered any before tonight."

Jos carried on. "I can only surmise that someone has got hold of some of my labels and attached them to the bottles."

"Nah! Not having it. You did it yourself. Very clever," said LaGarde, who had seemingly revoked his threat to leave the meeting.

Tedesco tried to suppress a smile. He had asked Jos to leave some unused wine labels on the table before the guests arrived. And he had noticed one member of the group taking several of them.

FORTY-SIX

The Trial Continues

Jos Elsted froze. Tedesco helped him.

"Do you want to respond?" he asked his friend.

"Yes. Of course, I didn't steam labels off some bottles of Madeira and attach my own. I'm not some sort of criminal mastermind. And wouldn't that have made me look guilty? Oh, and what would be my motive for killing three colleagues?"

Tedesco answered, as they had rehearsed. "You did have a motive when it came to Commander Foster though."

"Because I took over from him as head sidesman at the cathedral, after an open election? I think not!"

"People have killed for less," said Stephen Lowndes.

"No, they haven't, don't be bloody ridiculous," retorted Sylvia.

"But what about the other two? Verity and Poppy?" asked Tedesco.

"I would remind the court – meeting – that I am an openly gay man, so would have no romantic interest in either Verity or Poppy. I am also a very gentle man and abhor violence. Oh yes, and I can account for my movements at all relevant times."

Tedesco, sensing that his friend was in danger of overdoing the 'innocent man' thing, thanked Jos and said that he may have to return to his evidence when he summed up.

"Who shall I call next?" he asked, surveying the room.

"We haven't heard from Stephen and Rachel yet, or Dr Sue. Let's see – that still leaves Peter, Martin and Greville."

"We've heard plenty from that idiot already," huffed Sylvia.

"But we haven't sampled his wine choice, have we?"

Jos started to pour Greville Jackson's favourite, an Argentinian red from the hills of the Mendoza region, ably assisted in his task by Tony.

"Comments?" asked Tedesco, trying to balance his twin tasks of hosting a wine evening with acting as prosecutor. He would later reflect that this was a perfect example of the 'Wine and Crime' agency in practice.

"It's a bit heavy for me," said Mary Clayton.

"I think I will stick to my Stonker," was the considered verdict of Sylvia Spraggon.

"I rather like it," said Martin Smedley. "Rich, plummy."

"With notes of vanilla," added Rachel Lowndes.

"A bit short though," said her contrary husband, a comment that Tedesco filed away. He had more than a hunch that all was not well between those two.

Peter LaGarde kept his thoughts to himself, suspecting, correctly, that he would be next up.

Tedesco resumed his advocacy role.

"Well, Greville. Thank you for your choice. My wine of the evening so far. But turning to the murders, I think you have some questions to answer."

"I have a dog to feed!"

"So, let's speed things up, shall we? You live in Woolford, don't you?"

"You know I do! Gordon Bennett!"

"Thank you. And so do Jim and Mary Clayton."

"I see, so I broke into their shed and took the weed assassin or whatever it was called, and used it to bump off three people?"

Tedesco made another strategic pause, to let the witness stew.

"Actually, I don't think you did. I will come to that later."

He noticed Jackson's fellow Woolford residents Mark and Sue Elphick shifting uncomfortably in their seats.

Tedesco went on: "You have quite a collection of Madeira in your cellar, don't you, Greville?"

"You bloody well know that I do. I gave you a bottle at Christmas."

"Ah yes, your famous Christmas drinks parties. Would you care to comment on the fact that the only members of this club who didn't receive an invitation to your soirees are all dead?"

The members gave a collective gasp.

"That's not right! Smedley wasn't on the guest list either. Sorry, Smelly old chap, but I didn't want you ponging the house out. It's bad enough with Smollett letting off stink bombs all over the place."

"But Martin has received a threat, hasn't he? And I am satisfied that Sylvia has an alibi."

"Well done, Tedesco! You've got him bang to rights. I say we call it a night," said Peter LaGarde.

"Actually, Peter, do you mind if we sample your wine next? I have no more questions for Greville."

"Why not! You have proved it was him!"

"You will have to await my summing up. Tony, could you serve the next wine, please."

*

Those who had not made use of the spittoon were about to feel queasy. After sampling a light Beaujolais, two meaty reds and Sir Reggie Challenor's Madeira, vintage champagne was not, perhaps, the most obvious wine to serve next.

Peter LaGarde, true to his flamboyant public image, had selected Pol Roger, the supposed favourite of Winston Churchill.

Jos and Tony circled the room, carefully pouring a sample into some champagne flutes that Jos had hired for the evening.

"That's barely a mouthful!" shouted Sylvia. "Come on, fill her up!"

LaGarde, rather than commenting on the wine and its illustrious history, used the occasion to show off about the various parties he had hosted where the Pol Roger had flowed.

Dr Mark tried to interrupt him, stating that the champagne was sour and high-toned, while Greville Jackson opined that it was a grubby horror.

Peter brushed the comments aside.

Tedesco let him continue and then began to examine him. He decided that the direct approach was in order with this suspect.

"Peter, you are a wealthy man, something of a local success story, many would say."

"Wealthy? I'm hardly Elon Musk. But, yeah, by getting off my backside and grafting, I've done OK."

"Thank you. I understand that poor Poppy's funeral was arranged by Cockney Coffins?"

Jos noticed Greville Jackson shudder and mutter something about sheer vulgarity.

LaGarde looked genuinely puzzled by the line of questioning before it gradually dawned on him where this might be going.

"Yeah, they did. So what?"

"Bear with me. Is it correct that your father-in-law has a controlling interest in the firm? For the benefit of the meeting, Cockney Coffins is no ordinary funeral service. Thay have a huge share of the outer-London market. That's true, isn't it, Peter?"

Tedesco realised he was leading the witness, but, of course, it didn't matter.

This was a wine club, not a court of law.

"Peter?"

"Yes, it is. And I know what you are getting at. Poppy's old man left her a fortune, and you assume that I stand to get it."

"Won't you inherit from her?"

"Maybe. But we shared all we had anyway, so it won't make a penny of difference."

"A likely story!" barked Greville Jackson.

Tedesco steeled himself for his next question.

"Are you seeing anyone else, Peter? Someone you might be planning a new life with, for example. I have to ask."

"And I have to answer. No way."

Tedesco then stunned both LaGarde and the rest of the room by stating that he had no further questions.

Jos stood up. "I don't know about you, but I could do

with another tasting. Who haven't we heard from? How about Martin Smedley."

"Yeah, this should be a laugh," said Greville, who was surprisingly thin-skinned. He hadn't appreciated Martin's 'Squiffy' retort.

The put-upon archivist stood up and introduced his choice, an Austrian Gewürztraminer.

As the members paused to taste the wine, he explained that it was made from a single grape variety and that it had shifted his opinion.

"Unlike the widely available German offering, this has the sweetness of the grape but lacks that cloying quality."

"A bit like you, Martin," said Dr Sue, "sweet but not cloying."

"Give me strength," muttered Sylvia. "I'm getting popcorn mixed with molasses. It is foul!"

Jim and Mary Clayton stood up for Martin's choice, Mary suggesting that this would go down well at Christmas, while Stephen Lowndes said that if they were marking the wines he would have given it a seven plus.

Tedesco then reminded the room that this wasn't just a wine tasting, but a murder investigation.

"Martin, I think it would be fair to say that you have questions to answer about the death of Commander Foster."

"Really? I got on well with him, unlike most of you."

"How can I put this? When the Commander was discovered in his room, there was a particular odour present."

Poor Martin looked crestfallen.

"I don't know how many times I have to say this. It is a medical condition!"

"But this puts you in Foster's place around the time he died, doesn't it?"

Martin looked Tedesco in the eye, and then he took in the stares of the others in the room.

"I freely admit that I had been a regular visitor. As I told the police, Dr Sue was worried about the Commander and his mental health. He had taken the sidesman election very badly."

Dr Sue piped up. "I can confirm that. I was worried about Thomas, and I asked Martin if he could keep an eye on him for me. I was concerned that the Commander was cutting himself off from folk at the cathedral."

"Thank you, Dr Sue," said Tedesco, who had deliberately decided not to ask Martin if he had offered the Commander a lift to the tasting on the night he died.

"Is that it then?" Martin asked.

"Yes, it is, I am pleased to say. I cannot identify a motive for you, and Sue has confirmed that you visited Foster as an act of kindness. You may return to your seat."

Tedesco, Jos and Tony formed a little huddle, from which Jos emerged to make an announcement.

"We still have to sample the wines recommended by Stephen and Rachel, as well as Dr Sue. Looking at the time, could I suggest that we hear from one of you now and then have a ten-minute comfort break?"

Stephen Lowndes leapt to his feet, as Tedesco hoped he would.

"I'm happy to go next. My evidence won't take long."

Lowndes had chosen a supermarket own label wine, 'Good, Ordinary Claret'.

"Are you being an inverted snob or just a contrary little man?" asked Sylvia.

The schoolmaster ignored her and went on to describe the wine as doing what it said on the label.

"It's reliable, like a trusted car that never breaks down. And it's remarkably good value at under a tenner."

"You always were a stingy old miser," muttered his wife.

The other gluggers were surprisingly positive about his choice, influenced no doubt by the need for a comfort break.

"Now, Stephen," began Tedesco, "as Martin had questions to answer about Commander Foster, I think you have questions to answer about another of the victims. Verity Glynde. A bottle of poisoned Madeira was found in her apartment, and there was a card attached to the gift box which read 'All my love, Steve'. Were you in a relationship with Verity, Stephen?"

There was genuine shock in the room. Rachel broke the silence. "I always thought you were at it with that hippy, you bastard!"

Tony Camacho signalled for calm. The Big Man in black came into his own at times like these.

"Mr Lowndes?"

"Yes, we were friends. No more than that, although we both wanted more. We decided to bide our time."

"Were you conspiring to do away with me then?" shouted Rachel.

"Mrs Lowndes, you will have your chance after the break. And we are all looking forward to sampling your choice of wine. Now, Stephen. The card doesn't help your case, does it?"

"I admit that it doesn't look good, but I was at home when Verity died and – this is bloody embarrassing – Verity didn't call me Steve. We had pet names for each other."

"Give me strength," said Greville. Sylvia mimicked the act of retching into a bucket.

Stephen continued. "Verity's name for me was 'Doe Eyes', and I called Verity 'Lambkins.'"

Sylvia repeated the vomiting act.

"So why do you think that the card, ostensibly from you, was left with the Madeira?" asked Tedesco, once again flouting the rules of evidence.

"You need to ask her!" said Stephen, pointing at his wife.

"And that is what I will do, after our ten-minute break," Tedesco sums up.

While the gluggers queued for the loos, Tedesco checked with old Stander that the streaming had worked.

Then he called Jools at the station.

"I'm almost done."

"So I see. The streaming was a great idea. Do think you can get an admission? Or will it be several admissions?"

Tedesco laughed. "Patience, *ma brave*. Could you get here in about twenty minutes? I will time things as closely as I can. I assume you will be bringing the cavalry?"

"Jade and Matt are with me. Matt said it's like watching *Line of Duty*."

"I'm hurt, Jules. I am trying to be Hercule Poirot."

"See you in twenty."

As Tony called the meeting to order, Tedesco noticed Peter LaGarde once again glancing anxiously at his huge wristwatch.

"Thank you for your patience, ladies and gentlemen. I am confident that we are entering the home straight. Rachel, why don't you share your choice of wine."

"Well, it isn't poisoned Madeira! We are going to taste a Pinot noir from Romania, which I picked up on a business trip to a client over there, a Brit who has taken over much of the wine production. This is great value as well."

"I thought you said I was stingy," said Stephen.

Rachel ignored her husband and continued to enthuse about the raspberry taste and the soft tones.

The group, clearly in a hurry for the culprit or culprits to be unmasked, all made blandly positive comments.

Tedesco switched to investigative mode.

"What made you suspect that your husband was conducting a liaison with Verity?"

"He was always defending her at the meetings, and the way she batted her eyelashes at him – it couldn't have been more obvious."

"You decided to nip this is the bud, did you?"

"I wanted it to end, yes."

"So, you framed your husband?"

"Don't be absurd."

"You call him 'Steve', I assume?"

"Yes. So what?"

"Do you keep cards that he gives you on birthdays, special occasions?"

"Not really. I'm not sentimental."

"Nor are most serial killers," Mary Clayton whispered to Jim.

"I put it to you," said Tedesco, relishing the moment, "that you found an old card from your husband, cut out the message and then attached it to the gift box. You had motive and the means."

"What means?" said Rachel, thus implying acceptance that she might have had motive.

"You ordered the Weed Murderer, didn't you?"

"No."

"But you knew that the Claytons kept some in their shed, didn't you?"

The ice-cool architect started to cry. "Jim might have mentioned it, but it wasn't me. It wasn't me!"

Tedesco paused for effect. He was really enjoying this. Or was he guilty of showboating?

"I've heard enough," he said, sounding like Alan Sugar in the boardroom. "It's time for me to sum up."

The members visibly sat up, attention rapt.

"This has been a unique investigation in that everyone involved has fallen under suspicion. I can confirm that I am satisfied that neither Martin Smedley, Jos Elsted nor Sylvia Spraggon have committed murder. And nor have Jim or Mary."

"This is like when they announce who is going home in *Strictly*, isn't it, love," commented Jim Clayton.

"And it isn't us!" said a delighted Mary.

Tedesco tried to look a bit menacing, but it didn't really work.

"So that leaves Stephen and Rachel, Mark and Sue, Greville and Peter."

"Why don't you admit it, Rachel?" said Sylvia.

"Thank you for that intervention, Miss Spraggon. I am going to hand over to Jos at this point."

He took a gulp from a glass of water.

Jos, who couldn't even look a tiny bit menacing, turned to Rachel Lowndes.

"Rachel, John and I were both convinced that you had killed Verity and that you might have been involved in Poppy's death. We both wondered if you were having a fling with Peter, but we got that wrong as well. We are sure that the note – 'All my love, Steve' – was written by Stephen, and that it was intended for you. Did you have a birthday recently?"

"Yes, last week."

"But we accept that you didn't attach this to the Madeira. Someone else did."

Cue incredulous gasps from the audience.

"Greville. You have questions. Why did you choose to invite some of us to your Christmas party and not others? And doesn't it look just a bit suspicious that the ones you excluded have either been murdered or threatened that they will be next?"

Jackson grunted. "Have ever heard of the word 'coincidence', Elsted? I still think it was you."

"It wasn't. And why did you choose Madeira?"

"I have always done. It's a tradition at the Grange. Madeira for the staff."

"So that's how you see us, is it, the staff!" shouted a suddenly animated Dr Mark.

Tony stood up, which was enough to quell things.

Jos went on. "And you live in Woolford, of course. So, you could have siphoned off the weedkiller from Jim Clayton's shed, couldn't you?"

"I could have, but I bloody well didn't. You will be suggesting that Smollett helped me sniff it out next!"

"Did he?"

Tedesco reassumed his role as leading counsel.

"Greville, it's not you. All we have is circumstantial and although you are an infuriating snob, that doesn't make you a murderer. So that leaves Mark, Sue and Peter. I will keep this as short as I can. Mark, you have admitted that Poppy was one of your patients. You had a soft spot for her, didn't you?"

"Keep quiet, darling," said Sue. "Say 'no comment'."

"And, Peter, you suspected that Poppy was, as they put it

these days, 'playing away'. So, you embarked on a little frolic of your own, didn't you?"

"Now look here, Tedesco! I have warned you!"

"And your best mate is the chief constable, and you play golf with our member of parliament. Peter, I really don't care. And I think that it is high time that I unmasked the killer."

"Let the tumbrils sound!" shouted Sylvia.

"Shut up, you silly woman," said Martin Smedley, who had discovered his mojo.

"Hang on a minute," Jim Clayton interjected. "We haven't tried Sue's wine yet."

"And we won't," said Tedesco. "Because it was you, wasn't it, Dr Sue?"

FORTY-SEVEN

The Proof

Tedesco's analysis was spot on. Once he had summed up the case against her, Dr Sue would have no choice but to admit to the murders. All three of them.

She had suspected Mark, correctly, of having an affair with Poppy LaGarde.

Her own attempt at a retaliatory fling with Peter had been a bitter disappointment. LaGarde was more than happy to get into bed with her, momentarily turned on by the idea of an affair with an older married professional woman, but he was really only interested in sex, and he soon moved on to one of the receptionists at the health club.

Sue was desperate to get Mark back. He had fallen deeply in love with Poppy, and she knew it. She was going to lose him.

So, she hatched a complex plan. She knew that she could manipulate the members of the club, especially when they had been drinking.

The decision to kill Foster was taken to divert suspicion for the later murders.

The sozzled old fool was on his last legs. No one would really miss him.

She had encouraged Smedley to pay regular visits so that his odour – and prints – would be everywhere.

She very deliberately left a bottle of the Madeira at the house when she gave Foster a lift to the meeting and she even told him to make sure that he had a glass of the wine before he went to sleep, telling him that she had read a recent article in *The Lancet* which extolled the medicinal properties of the stuff.

And as for motive, Jos would come under suspicion after his ousting of the Commander from his office at the cathedral and for the presence of his name on the bottle, as would Greville after his spat with him at the tasting.

Add Smedley to the mix and there was a complex investigation to be had – and no one would suspect her.

Rachel Lowndes had confided to her good friend Dr Sue about her suspicions concerning Verity, so Sue took full advantage of the information. She found out from patient records that Rachel had an imminent birthday and went round with a card and an expensive bouquet.

While Rachel left the sitting room to put the flowers in water, Sue went through the cards on the mantelpiece and took down the one from Stephen.

She had some scissors in her bag and swiftly cut off the signature. Rachel was not sentimental and the day after her birthday she chucked her birthday cards into the blue recycling bin. She never noticed that the card had been tampered with.

In the meantime, Sue had stopped off, en route from the hospital, to drop the card and present at Verity's flat in the Cathedral Close.

She did have a stroke of luck – one of the old dears from

the neighbouring apartments had taken it in for her and left it in the communal area for Verity to pick up when she returned home.

Sue's plan worked. Verity drank a glass of the Madeira later that evening, with fatal results. And the web that Sue was weaving was becoming ever more tangled.

The members had fallen silent during Tedesco's masterly exposition. Greville Jackson broke the silence.

"This is all very clever, Tedesco. Bravo and all that. But I still can't believe that it was Sue."

Sue, tearful, confessed that it was she who had committed the murders, and that Tedesco had reached the correct conclusion.

"Hang on," said Martin Smedley. "How did you get hold of the poison, Dr? I can't imagine you breaking into the shed. I still can't believe you did all this, to be honest."

Mary Clayton spoke up. "Sue and Mark had a spare set of keys to the house and the shed. Sue, how could you?!"

Tedesco calmly told the meeting that the Claytons had explained to the police early in the investigation that the doctors had been given the spare set so they could keep an eye on the house when they were away. He had put this to the back of his mind, distracted by the various theories as to who had ordered the Weed Murderer from Jim, but when he had been going through his case notes, he was reminded of this. As he often told himself, it's the little facts that solve cases.

"The keys to the mystery, you might say," said Stephen Lowndes, who was looking devastated. His feelings for Verity were genuine and he was already wondering if it was too late to save his marriage, or if he even wanted to.

"I'm sorry," Greville said, "but I still have doubts about

you, Elsted. You haven't explained about how your labels were attached to the bottles."

"I will take that," said Tedesco, turning to Dr Sue. "Jos left some blank labels on the table tonight to see if anyone took them, and I saw Sue put them in her bag. This isn't the first time you have done that, is it?"

Sue nodded. She had taken some of Jos's labels from his office and had stuck them on old wine bottles, having carefully steamed off the old labels.

"But what about Poppy? How did you bump her off?" asked the ever-sensitive Sylvia.

Tedesco gestured to Tony, who left the meeting. The police would be here any minute so the Big Man could deal with them. Then he continued.

"Having created several smokescreens by murdering Foster and Verity, Sue turned to the person she really wanted dead all along. This will be difficult for you to hear, Peter, I am so sorry. And I guess this isn't easy for you either, Mark."

LaGarde's trademark pomposity had deflated during the evening, like a slow puncture. He just shrugged his shoulders and gestured for Tedesco to continue. Dr Mark put his head in his hands.

"I would ask those of you who attended Commander Foster's wake to cast your minds back to that fateful occasion. What do you remember about the wine?"

Mary Clayton broke the silence. "It was a white, I think. Rather unusual."

"It was an interesting choice," confirmed Jos. "And I recently recalled that I had discussed which wines to serve with the club secretary. Am I right, Sue?"

She nodded in weary agreement.

"It was an Italian Zinfandel. Chosen, John and I now know, because of how it might react with cyanide. The lab tests confirmed it."

"All well and good, Elsted, but the others were bumped off with Madeira," said Greville Jackson.

"And this was a problem. I assumed that there were two killers, one who had used Madeira and the other who had chosen the Zinfandel as the agent of death. But then we had a lucky breakthrough, didn't we, Jos?"

The wine merchant cleared his throat. "I assume that we are all familiar with Julie Stringer?"

"That ghastly woman from the local rag!" said Sylvia.

"Her column is absolute bile," said Greville.

"Anyway, Julie called at our offices in Minster Precincts recently. She sometimes makes these unscheduled appearances to see if we have any scraps of gossip."

"And it is always a wasted journey for her, as we are totally committed to client confidentiality," Tedesco swiftly added.

"Thank you for that, John. On this occasion, Julie had something for us. She said that it probably wasn't important, but she had suffered a flashback to the afternoon of the wake. Actually, why don't we hear from the lady herself?"

Tony Camacho escorted Julie, who looked delighted to be in his company, from the kitchen where she had been waiting to make her grand entrance. DC Jade Sennen had prearranged to collect her once Tedesco was ready to reveal the killer.

Tedesco hoped that Julie hadn't heard the unkind comments coming from Sylvia and Greville, but later reflected that she had probably heard worse, and that she possessed the hide of an especially tough rhinoceros.

The hard-bitten journalist swept into the meeting and was given a seat at the head of the table.

Tedesco made a more formal introduction before thanking her for her time at such short notice.

"Julie, could you please tell the court – sorry, the meeting! – what you told Jos and I about the wake for Commander Foster."

The witness responded confidently.

"I had always thought that the only people serving the food and drink at the wake were the staff – of the refectory, that is."

There was much head nodding from the others.

"But then I remembered that I saw Dr Sue handing out drinks to some of the guests."

"And did this include Poppy LaGarde, do you remember?"

"Yes."

Dr Sue interrupted, "You can all save your breath. I did hand out wine, but only to the Glug, Glug members. I am club secretary, and so it was plausible that I might be interested in the members' opinions."

"But did you hand the wine to Poppy?" asked Jos.

"I did."

"Now," said Jos, warming to his role as junior counsel, "I remember my learned friend Mr Tedesco commenting that the wine left in Poppy's glass looked effervescent. Do you have anything to say about that, Dr Sue?"

Sue's customary air of competence almost visibly faded. "Alright! Alright! I had laced the Zinfandel in Poppy's glass with some granules of the weedkiller. I almost gave her the wrong glass but noticed just in time."

"I remember that," said Peter. "I nearly took it! I wish I had now, you evil—"

Tedesco told him to be quiet as he had a further question for Sue. It was about the message 'WHIFFY. YOU ARE NEXT.'

Sue ruefully admitted to having delivered the death threat to Martin Smedley, as a final – as it turned out – desperate attempt to muddy the waters.

DCI Tagg, DS Lovell and DC Sennen suddenly broke into the meeting and arrested Dr Sue, who went quietly. Her expression conveyed relief above anything else.

While Lovell and Sennen drove Sue away, Jools stayed behind, thanking all concerned for their help in bringing the culprit to justice.

"How did you know this was going to happen? Bit of a coincidence, you arriving at the precise moment of her confession," said Jim Clayton.

"There was an element of subterfuge," said Tedesco. "Can I ask Mr Stander to join us? He has been live-streaming the whole event, so he deserves a drink!"

"Rather underhand, don't you think?" said Martin Smedley.

"I reckon we could all do with a snorter," said Greville. "I just happen to have brought a bottle of Madeira…"

FORTY-EIGHT

Wash Up

Tony didn't make it back to 17 St Budeaux Place that night.

"Do you think we should report him as a missing person, Barker? No, you are probably right. My money is on Julie. Tony is flying back to Madeira in a couple of days' time, so I am sure he will be back in the morning. He might be a bit tired after a night on the tiles with our favourite journalist though."

As the border terrier trotted off to his basket, his master poured himself a glass of Côtes du Rhône.

He needed something relatively light to ease him to sleep after his tour de force at the meeting.

He reflected that Glug, Glug had probably held its last tasting, at least for a long while, and that two marriages – those of Stephen and Rachel and Mark and Sue – had irretrievably broken down. Peter had lost his wife, but Tedesco, somewhat harshly for him, felt that the inheritance of her Cockney Coffins fortune would go some way towards softening the blow. A man like Peter LaGarde wouldn't be on his own for long. And he could always adopt another alias.

Greville Jackson and Sylvia Spraggon would continue their relentless competition for the title of rudest person in Rhyminster, the Claytons would resume their old sweet ways and Martin Smedley would bury himself back in the archives.

He wondered if he and Jos would be in demand as DCI Tagg had told him that they would be given public recognition for their work in unmasking that most unlikely multiple murderer, Dr Susan Elphick.

As he refilled his glass, he thought of Tony. He was the kind of person who, once the connection had been made, had the habit of popping up in the unlikeliest places. He felt sure that he would see him again. He hoped so.

Time for a last track. He was stuck at that awkward crossroads between sentimental and maudlin and was thinking about his youth and childhood in Plymouth. He needed to go back. Soon. Confront the ghosts.

He removed the album cover with an almost religious reverence, dusted the vinyl and carefully placed it on the turntable.

The song was by Van Morrison. The title, 'Memory Lane'.

He silently toasted the singer and awarded the song a ten.

WHO'S WHO IN THE JOHN TEDESCO SERIES

John Tedesco

Profession: Private Detective

After a difficult childhood in Plymouth, with a largely absent father who was both a non-commissioned officer in the Royal Navy and a functioning alcoholic, John and his sister were brought up by their hard-pressed but saintly mother Marcia. With her support, he made it to grammar school and then to the University of Exeter, where he read law.

After a successful career as a solicitor in Rhyminster, culminating in his appointment as legal adviser to the bishop, he formed his detective agency with Lynne Davey, a previous client and ex-CID officer.

He is now acknowledged as a leading expert in ecclesiastical investigation.

Although he is a born romantic, he has never married. His one true love, Irish bookseller Sorcha, died of cancer in 2022.

Likes: his work; Plymouth Argyle Football Club; his Lancia car; good wine; gentle early seventies music – think James Taylor, Carole King – and English cathedrals.

Dislikes: Exeter City football club; rappers; political extremism; rudeness; travelling beyond Devon and Cornwall – but Madeira may turn out to be the exception to the rule.

Distrusts: The rapid rise of technology.

Best friend: Barker. He is also close to his sister Nicky.

Other significant friends: Lynne, his former business partner; Canon Wilfred; Jos Elsted.

Barker

Adorable border terrier who is loved by his master; the feeling is mutual

As well as performing highly in his role as mental health champion to the detective agency, he has unearthed many crucial pieces of evidence for Tedesco, but he is very modest about it.

Likes: a run on his favourite beach; snuggling up by the fire while his master pours himself a glass of wine and plays his music. Barker prefers Chopin or Bach but has developed a taste for the singer-songwriter genre.

Dislikes: anyone who treats his master with less than respect; aggressive dogs and humans; the ringtone on Tedesco's phone; the hoover.

Tolerates: Being stroked in the wrong way; Tedesco's PA – she really is a bit ditsy.

Canon Wilfred Drake

Profession: canon precentor at Rhyminster Cathedral

This role places him at the heart of worship and music at the ancient building.

Canon Wilfred is a traditionalist in his music, intolerant of anything composed after the late seventeenth century, let alone the stuff his friend John loves.

However, his approach to the Church is anything but stuck in the past. He is a quiet supporter of same-sex marriage and is highly critical of church hierarchy, especially over safeguarding issues. This criticism has probably held him back, but he is no careerist. Tedesco thinks he is the last of the old-fashioned pastoral priests.

Likes: choral evensong; sharing a pot of tea with Tedesco in the refectory; people, they are endlessly fascinating and often surprising. He is a fully paid-up member of Barker's fan club.

Dislikes: aggressive atheists and born-again Christians – they are different sides of the same coin to Wilfred and exhibit a terrifying certainty that only they are in the right.

Friends: a countless number. However, he is very close to Tedesco and has acted as his unofficial spiritual adviser, ably assisted by Barker, of course.

Sally Munks

Profession: PA to the detective agency based at 4A Minster Precincts

From day one, Sally is at the heart of the building from when she arrives on her pushbike, laden with various jute bags containing who knows what, to when she cycles home every evening at the stroke of 5pm on the cathedral clock.

A voracious charity fundraiser and volunteer, she can drive Tedesco mad with her various good causes, but he has often been heard to say that society relies on the goodwill of people like Sally and that there should be more people like her.

Likes: a good rummage, whether through her carrier bags or at a jumble sale; her two book clubs; spending time with friends at Rhyminster Arts Centre; scented candles; Barker.

Dislikes: climate-change deniers; drivers of large polluting cars.

Tolerates: her boss when he is in one of his touchy moods.

Friends: Sally sees the whole of creation as her friend.

DCI Julia 'Jools' Tagg
Profession: Detective Chief Inspector

Jools was the protégé of Lynne Davey, Tedesco's original business partner and former-CID officer.

A local girl, Jools has risen through the ranks and is highly regarded. However, although unflappable and decisive, she is not overburdened with personal ambition. She loves her work but would hate to move from Rhyminster.

Jools has used her friend Tedesco to assist her with investigations on several occasions.

Likes: socialising; cold-water swimming; mentoring her own protégé, Jade Sennen.

Dislikes: interference from above, especially if it comes from outside her patch; The Boys' Club.

Would like: a stable relationship – she has sometimes wished that Tedesco was twenty or thirty years younger.

Secret ambition: to train as a silversmith.

Jocelyn 'Jos' Elsted
Profession: wine merchant

Jos moved to Rhyminster after the death of his long-term partner. He needed to get away from London and sought sanctuary in the Cathedral Close in Rhyminster, where he maintains a beautifully furnished apartment.

Although he has encountered prejudice from the likes of

Commander Foster, the openly gay Jos has become a well-known and popular figure in the little cathedral city.

His wine business has expanded into new premises in the same building as those of Tedesco's detective agency and this has cemented their friendship.

As Tedesco is knowledgeable about wine, and as Jos has displayed some unexpected investigative skills in previous instalments of the Rhyminster novels, the two men have entered an informal alliance, which they refer to as 'Crime and Wine'.

Likes: throwing catered dinner parties, making full use of his lovely home; attending fine-art auctions; keeping in touch with his customers, many of whom have become friends.

Dislikes: all forms of ignorance and prejudice.

Something surprising: since moving to Rhyminster, Jos has gradually found faith. After bravely leading a walk-out during the late bishop's anti-woke and clearly homophobic sermon, he was overwhelmed by the support he received from the cathedral community. He has been chosen, to his amazement, as the head sidesman, responsible for the volunteers who steward the services.

Nicola 'Nicky' Tedesco

Profession: broadcast journalist

Left school at eighteen to work on the ads desk at the *Plymouth Herald* before joining the local BBC station, where she has been a reporter for over twenty years. Nicky is a regular presenter of the evening magazine programme, *Searchlight Tonight*.

After an acrimonious divorce from her husband Jeremy 'Chag' Wills, the family home near Rhyminster was sold and she bought a plush apartment at Royal William Yard, Plymouth, so she can be near the studio.

Although Tedesco misses her living close at hand, he is delighted to see the back of Chag Wills and is thrilled to see Nicky enjoying life as a newly independent woman.

Likes: intelligent conversation; singing in a local choir; cooking; foreign travel; being asked to house-sit when John is away. Nicky is another Barker fan.

Dislikes: team sports, especially rugby – Chag was a rugby obsessive; having to do the late news shift; being recognised in local restaurants but accepts that it is part of the job.

Regrets: staying in the marriage for the sake of the children – Nicky is determined to make up for lost time.

Misses: Jack and Ella, but they are both good at keeping in touch and have turned into well-rounded adults. Jack flirted with far-right politics in his late teens but is completely over it. She also misses her brother; they will always look out for each other.

DS Matthew Lovell

Profession: Detective Sergeant

A quiet stalwart presence in the Tedesco novels, Matt is the able assistant and foil to Julia Tagg. An uncomplicated type, he is surprisingly vain about his appearance. Married to Sue, with two small children, Luke and Amelia. He tends to compartmentalise, keeping his home life separate from his work.

Likes: family life; when he can, he enjoys a pint or two with his old mates at Rhyminster Rugby Club.

Dislikes: entitled civilians – the expressions 'Don't you know who I am, Officer?' and 'I play golf with the chief constable' are particularly irritating to him.

<u>Surprising fact:</u> he achieved grade eight at the piano.

Julie Stringer

Profession: print journalist

Something of a local legend due to her long-running 'It Makes Me Mad!' column in the *Rhyminster Journal*, Julie has been a mild irritant to Tedesco over the years.

Her tendency to indiscretion has threatened to derail various investigations.

<u>Likes:</u> a good gossip; dishing the dirt with her girlfriends; any excuse for a celebration; champagne; clothes shopping.

<u>Specialist skill:</u> flirting with anyone, from the bishop to the binman.

<u>Dislikes:</u> peace and quiet; an empty social diary; the minority of men who prove impervious to her voluptuous charms; being underestimated.

<u>Little-known fact:</u> before training as a journalist, Julie read modern languages at Bristol and is fluent in French and Spanish.

The city of Rhyminster

This is an invented place, sitting roughly where Totnes lies in the South Hams district of Devon.

The smallest cathedral city in England, fictional Rhyminster contains elements of three real cathedral cities, Salisbury, Wells and Winchester, as well as of Totnes itself.

The villages of Woolford and Derrington are entirely fictional.

ACKNOWLEDGEMENTS

Thanks as always to all my readers, whether you buy, borrow or download.

I hope that Tedesco's return has lived up to expectations.

On the wine side, I must mention SWIG (Salisbury Wine Interest Group) for their varied tastings and for harbouring a writer in their midst, and the Real Wine Company and Artisan Wine and Spirits, Salisbury for their excellent selections. Both come strongly recommended by Jos Elsted. Praise doesn't come any higher.

On the personal front, I couldn't do this without the support of Lucinda, my lovely wife. She is my first reader and honest critic, as well as my IT consultant. I am truly blessed.

ABOUT THE AUTHOR

Radu was brought up in Plymouth, Devon, before his family moved to Hampshire.

His well-received memoir, *Home Park Heaven: A Plymouth Childhood* was published by Troubador earlier this year.

He practised law for over thirty years and continues to help out with holiday cover at his former practice in Winchester.

When not writing, he can be found at Salisbury Cathedral, where he guides and stewards, or at Arundells, the home of former prime minister Sir Edward Heath, where he is a room steward.

Like John Tedesco, he continues to follow Plymouth Argyle Football Club, travelling to Home Park as often as he can, and cheers on his local non-league side, Salisbury FC, when a free Saturday afternoon coincides with a home game.

This book is printed on paper from sustainable sources managed under the Forest Stewardship Council (FSC) scheme.

It has been printed in the UK to reduce transportation miles and their impact upon the environment.

For every new title that Troubador publishes, we plant a tree to offset CO_2, partnering with the More Trees scheme.

For more about how Troubador offsets its environmental impact, see www.troubador.co.uk/sustainability-and-community